The One Just South of Paradise

By T.X. O'Kelley

Published by

◢ köehlerbooks™

3705 Shore Drive
Virginia Beach, VA 23455
800–435–4811
www.koehlerbooks.com

The ONE
Just SOUTH *of*
PARADISE

T.X. O'Kelley

VIRGINIA BEACH
CAPE CHARLES

To my mother, Patty Ann, who taught me to love books,
beauty, faith, and truth.

CHAPTER 1

I COULD ONLY FIND HIM there, on the one just south of paradise. So, when I most needed him in my fourteenth summer, I went to the cay. To see him squint at sunrise and sunset on the high porch. To hear how wind and tide would change our day. To learn how to tie a proper blood knot. To see if he could hear me when I didn't speak at all.

No one else had heard me that year, though I had been very loud. I had spoken out in class in ways passionate and incoherent. When I told Sister Mary Veronica that God probably didn't exist, I had not shouted. But the volume seemed sufficient to be heard.

I had certainly used plenty of volume with my mother as I told her that she did not understand anything about me, and that we were completely different. I know I was loud when I told her she'd probably wasted her life as a house Frau.

I knew that last one had hit home. It was a direct quote from my friend Deborah Cooley. Actually, from Deborah's older sister Wendy. I'd always admired Wendy. She was four years ahead of us. She was thin, chic, and gorgeous. And tired. She'd always seemed tired, especially of our little world in Fort Lauderdale. She was a freshman at NYU, and she kept Deborah and I posted on heroin chic, feminist theory, and the obvious wisdom of atheism. She smoked and talked, and I'd soaked it up, feeling big enough to be at ease in the bonus room above their garage on the beanbag chairs, looking up at the Che Guevara posters.

I'd tried reading Simone de Beauvoir. Though I secretly couldn't get through it, I had enough for a few choice phrases. When short on reasons, I also tried tears and screams and scenes to make these points. I tried raising the volume on my father too, but he had only looked at me, there in the kitchen, fixing me with his very blue eyes. He clearly hadn't heard me, or he would have reacted or said something more than "You need to collect yourself, Kit. Let me know when you want to have a real conversation. I'll be there."

So, I came to the cay, because there was no more there for my dad than that spit of sand, rock, and palm just off the northern edge of Andros Island.

My mother put me on a small plane at Fort Lauderdale Executive with thinly disguised relief and a lilt in her voice, saying, "Enjoy the cay, darling!"

Dad collected me at the tarmac, metal huts that served as the North Andros Airport. I climbed into our weathered blue Suburban with my canvas bag adorned with a huge, hand-scrawled peace sign. He was quiet for a mile or so as we sped north on the long, straight ribbon of pocked blacktop that is the Queen's Highway. I stared out at the stands of pines and savannah grass. I opened my window and felt the hot salt air.

"Been a little warm. Bugs bad. Fishing's terrific. You know, the usual summer conditions."

I nodded and gave an "Uh-huh."

He looked straight on again, and after five more miles of blacktop, we were on the old sand road snaking through thick pines to the coral rock edge of the island and the dock. We threw my bag into the skiff and pushed out. I could see the cay and the high white house, framed by broad porches and pale-blue hurricane shutters, open now to what little breeze stirred.

Sebastian was there on the dock, barefoot, under an old ball cap. I still don't know exactly how old he was. Perhaps ten or fifteen years older than my father, who must've been forty-three or forty-four that year. Sebastian, tall and lean as a two-by-four and coal black from a lifetime in the Bahamas sun and from his ancestor, an African slave who'd jumped ship in the strait and swam ashore six generations before. Sebastian could dive and fish and fix anything, and he could even cook. I think only I knew that he did not actually like to do this last thing, yet he would do it without complaint if asked by my parents or his wife, Veronica.

"Look how grown up!" He took my bag and gave me a one-armed hug. Even sweet Sebastian could offend me that summer. I heard "grown out," not *up*, thinking of my suddenly growing back end and ridiculous budding chest and body that suddenly seemed as unfamiliar as alien abduction. But I could not growl at Sebastian.

"Yes, I know. Thank you. Glad to be back."

This last thing was untrue. My mother had suggested a week on the cay with my father as just the thing for my "blue temper." I'd kind of wanted to go, but at the last minute, a frantic series of calls from Monica Diaz had turned my head to a pool party and quinceañera right in the middle of that time. I couldn't miss it. Everyone would be there. But my mother insisted that plans had been made. The pool party would be missed. It was, I thought, typical of her to completely fail to understand me, or anything about my life—or for that matter, anything in this decade. I'd let her know about her lack of understanding again that morning in the car. I must not have cleared up the signs of my regret.

As we crossed the porch, Dad looked at me and said, "You okay, Kit? Looks like someone shot your dog." This was his old query for any appearance of sadness in his children. He got me settled in my room, flicking on the light.

"Yeah, I'm good." My mom would have pressed on from there. But he gave nothing.

"Okay. Get settled. We'll see about lunch in a bit."

And he was gone. He was down in the shed, tinkering with fishing gear and an old boat engine, then reading in the big wicker chair on the veranda. Two hours passed on the cay with nothing but the hush of the gently swelling breakers over the reef, and the tinny sound of Nassau radio in the kitchen.

I unpacked. I lay on my old bed. I ran my finger along the line of books on the shelf. The photos of an eight- and ten-year-old me looked like a different girl. I felt sad for her, unsteady. I closed my eyes.

He called me for lunch. Veronica had sent out some chowder for us. Food had gotten complicated. But conch chowder seemed okay. Especially Veronica's, which I loved. But I promised myself no johnnycake as I went into the kitchen.

It was good, and I ate the whole bowl. I broke my promise and had a piece of johnnycake but skipped the butter. We'd been pretty quiet during lunch. I told Dad the basics of home over the last few weeks. Mom's tennis and decorating. My older brothers' summer jobs. I asked him about Veronica.

"She's pretty good. Her mom's been sick, so that's been hard. But otherwise, good."

When he asked about school in the fall, I told him I was dreading it. I laid out how claustrophobic Our Lady of Mt. Carmel Academy had gotten. The gossipy girls. The pettiness of the rules. The tyranny of Sister Mary Veronica. At the mention of my nemesis, he chuckled.

"Don't you think it's a little ironic that, on one side of the Gulf Stream, you have a Veronica you can't stand, and on the other side, one you love?"

The shared name had occurred to me, but I'd gone no further. The chilly sister had nothing in common with the warm and funny Veronica here on Andros.

Dad continued, "They're both about the same age, I bet."

I had no idea how old Sister was. Mom said you couldn't tell because the habit covered their hair.

"They couldn't be more different, Dad."

He looked out at the veranda and the water beyond.

"Yeah, I suppose. But maybe more alike than you realize. Both hard workers, both good at keeping things running, both living their lives for the people around them."

"Veronica would never treat me like Sister does."

"She might if she was in charge of your education. She can be pretty tough. You see how she talks to Malcolm and Freddy."

I had indeed seen Veronica loudly scold her two sons many times.

Dad looked at me now. "It's because she knows they can be something special. It's her job to make sure they get there." He raised his eyebrows and grinned a little.

Then he was up, rinsing the bowls, and I got busy putting the food away. I had one more thumb full of johnnycake while I put it in Saran wrap.

A thunderstorm moved through that afternoon, and the wind blew through the shutters. We read, and I slept for a while. By late afternoon, the storm was a tower of black moving toward Florida. The cay and reef beyond were bathed in the green-gold light that switches on after a big storm passes. I had my sketch pad out on the porch.

"No human has ever captured that light."

He peered over my shoulder.

"Maybe you're the one."

"Not me." I kept my eyes on my pad.

"You can't know yet. You're only starting. You have to see how good you can be."

He raised his eyes and peered at the sketch: "I like the line on Fish Cay. That big palm at the end, and then the rock, runs into the water just like that." He nodded to himself and out at the distant cay and then walked away.

After dinner, we played dominoes, and he smoked a cigar on the porch. After a while, I went out and sat with him. The stars were so big and bright, they looked like they might fall on us at any moment.

"I thought we'd fish the falling tide tomorrow."

"What time?"

"Not too early. Out around eight."

This was a mercy. Dad was not afraid to rise long before first light to catch a tide.

"Sounds good."

"How's the casting?"

He expected me and my brothers to practice our fly-casting. Even in Fort Lauderdale. In the yard. I had not practiced in some time. But I still said, "Fine."

"Good. Shouldn't be much wind tomorrow."

No wind meant easy casting. I knew then that he knew I had not been practicing.

CHAPTER 2

I HEARD HIM up before the sun and smelled coffee and bacon. I drifted back to sleep, then woke to the sound of Sebastian's voice. They were on the veranda, talking the way they did—Sebastian's deep voice and heavy Andros accent rumbling between long pauses, Dad barely audible, still asking questions after all their years fishing together.

"That's because bonefish doesn't like all that hard current and the water stirred up on outgoing."

I did not hear Dad's question, but I knew this was the answer.

I dressed and came out to see them standing at the big table on the veranda. There were bonefish flies spilled out on the table and the remains of breakfast and coffee cups.

"Good morning, Kit." I had come to dislike my babyish nickname very much because I was Catherine now. I had not hesitated to correct classmates, teachers, and my mother. But I would not correct Sebastian.

"Morning."

"Are you ready to catch some fish?"

He seemed very happy. So I told a small white lie, "Yes, very."

I was not ready—in my casting or my enthusiasm.

"Good. Your dad needs help. We need a change in our luck."

I looked at Dad, and he was smiling, raising his eyebrows.

"I thought it had been good?"

Sebastian shook his big head topped with gray. "Lots of fish, but soft mouth."

I knew this meant they were not taking the fly. Not interested. Not hungry, perhaps.

He looked at me and smiled. "So, you'll bring the change. You've always been good luck."

I had not heard this before and was not sure I believed it. I looked at the flies on the table. Tiny bundles of bright feathers, silvery bodies, lead pop eyes, all meant to look like an enticing shrimp.

"So, what are we using this morning?"

Dad said, "You choose, Kit. We'll be starting off Little Hog Cay. The big flat. White bottom. Falling tide."

I really had no idea. But it was a mild test. Just to choose was enough.

I picked one up, and felt the soft feathers, the tight body. I pressed my finger against the sharp hook concealed beneath.

"How about the Gotcha?"

It was the only one I could surely recall by name. I hoped I was either holding one or looking at one. I was lucky.

"Always a good choice." Sebastian smiled and nodded. Dad smiled too.

I never ceased to thrill at the run out to the flats—sitting in the front of the skiff, engine roaring, speeding over turquoise water in the early-morning light, passing the pink and green pastel cottages of Lowe Sound far off to our left, and catching the ragged green line on the horizon of Hawk Cay, then Fish, then Hog. Feeling the boat skim and turn, holding tight in the seat, Sebastian worked his way through the narrow channels of deep blue between white sand flats. I was in fleece for the cool run of the morning, though it would be ninety degrees by midday.

The engine idled back, then slowly crept along as Dad and Sebastian stood and looked for fish.

"There. Fish all in there."

I followed Sebastian's pointing arm and saw the dark mass with tiny points flashing in the morning sun. Dad nodded.

Sebastian spoke quietly. "They waiting on the tide. We'll start at this end with the water and walk in."

Dad agreed. Sebastian staked the boat at the end of the flat, a few hundred yards from the school of bonefish.

We would begin our stalk here.

"Kit, you fish with me. Your dad doesn't need me anymore."

Dad laughed. "Hardly. But I'll do my best."

Dad did not need a guide anymore, but he and Sebastian fished as one after all these years.

I stepped off into the knee-deep water, cold on my khakis and running shoes. I gathered my fly rod, and Sebastian set off a few steps in front of me. He wore an old cotton shirt, work khakis, and the same faded, blue ball cap he'd had on the day before. He walked with one arm behind him, leaning forward, slowly, methodically, barefoot, like a bonefishing Sherlock Holmes.

After a minute, he turned to me and pointed to my feet. "Not so hard. Softly."

It was a common thing for him to tell me. Having danced ballet since I was big enough to walk, I still never knew what he meant, or how one could walk a sand flat less hard. But I nodded anyway and willed myself lighter.

As we neared the fish, we slowed. I could see them now, dark silhouettes like torpedoes, huddled together, all facing us, barely moving in the tide. Tiny points of silver flashed in the pack, as tail and fin just above the water's surface caught the sunlight. Dad was to our right, crouching slightly now as he edged closer. I saw a large, dark shadow glide in front of the pack of fish, its tail swaying in rhythm. A small shark.

Sebastian grunted. "He waiting for you to catch his breakfast. Them too."

He pointed at two smaller sharks circling on the backside of the pack.

"You'll have to reel fast." He motioned with his hands to show a tight line pulling in.

We were a mere twelve yards away now, and the fish were still.

He turned to me and quietly said, "Okay. Put one front left of them."

I pulled more line from the reel and took the rod back. My heart pounded. I swung it forward, short, then back.

"Take your time. Slowly." He was trying to help, but I wanted only to say, "I know." I could not get the line back far enough. I swung hard forward. The line dropped less than ten feet in front of me, a hopeless puddle of bright yellow.

"Too short. Try again." I knew it was too short. I hadn't even really casted. I wanted to tell him. But I pulled out the line and swung it back and forth again.

"Slow down."

I knew it was too fast, but I swung it harder. I could get it there. The line fell ten feet in front of the fish.

"Too short. Try again."

I wanted to hand the rod to him, to have him cast it for me like he did when I was little, then let me catch the fish. But he was not looking at me. He stared at the fish, willing them to stay.

I saw Dad. He wasn't casting. He was waiting, leaning forward,

me through his sunglasses. He smiled and nodded at me

his hand slightly with a thumbs-up. I pulled in the line.

raised his arm high above his head and swept it back and

ly now. Take your time."

ught the rod high and back and looked for the big *S* of line

nd Dad had taught me was the sign of a proper false cast.

w, then on the third, Sebastian said, "Just let it go."

. And the line shot out. It was left and a little short. But it

ugh. I saw a fish move toward it. I heard Sebastian's loud

, "Rod tip down. Strip."

lled the line through my fingers.

"Not so hard. Smooth. Strip. Strip. Keep stripping."

I pulled again, and then again. I saw the tail tip up and felt the fish tugging.

"Strip." I pulled again.

Fish on. A bolt of silver splash, then churning water, then line singing through my fingers and off the reel.

"Let him run now." Then he shouted, "Now she's fishing, Doc!"

And he was happy.

"Tight line now. He's done running." I reeled in crazy, wobbly, trying to keep the slack out. Then I felt him like a concrete block in a washing machine, tumbling, ripping, pulling.

"Don't fight him now. Let him run again. Shark okay." Sebastian was watching the big lemon for me to make sure he didn't take the fish. He ran again, big and fast and silvery. Then swung hard and steady left. When he slowed, Sebastian said, "Catch him now." And I reeled again crazy, quickly, now more smoothly. And then he was at our feet. Sebastian splashed swiftly forward and grabbed the leader.

He was big and beautiful, shiny, and fierce.

"Nice fish. Very nice."

Dad was there now.

"Picture, Kit."

I wet my hands in the water and held the fish, and Dad snapped the photo of me and my fish and Sebastian. Sebastian quickly took the hook out and moved him through the water gently, reviving him. And then he was gone.

Sebastian laughed and smiled broadly.

"That was a nice fish. Best fish all week."

He was walking away now. I looked at Dad.

"Really?"

"Well, I had a couple pretty good ones."

Sebastian did not turn. "No, that one was the best."

Dad laughed and shook his head.

Sebastian called out over his shoulder, "Come on, Doc, let's see if you can catch a fish."

They had moved past us, and we had to circle around in a wide stalk to keep the sun behind us.

I cast at the edges but missed short. I tangled my line on my rod tip twice. Dad got one to take off the right edge of the pack. He brought it in quickly and cleanly and took it off himself. He smiled from across the flat widely enough for us to see. He held up his hands with the span of a large fish.

The fish broke up then. Sebastian stood tall and moved back toward the boat.

"They gone now."

I looked around and saw suddenly that he was right. I had no idea where that many fish could have disappeared to in the wide flat of gin-clear water. But they were gone.

We moved further north to another flat, and the wind picked up. It was not blowing hard, but in my mind, it howled. Sebastian put it to our backs. I tried to cast still harder.

"Slow down. Big S." I just got quicker.

The fish were moving now into the falling tide. I needed to put the fly just in front of them. I couldn't see them now, the water a sheen of cloud cover and ripples. Sebastian told me where they were, with the directions of the clockface and distance in feet. But I still could not see them. I missed. Too short.

" Try again." I heard that for what seemed like the hundredth time that morning. I pulled up at the rod tip and yanked the line, and it ripped from the water. The fish scattered in a splashing, urgent flight.

Sebastian watched them go. "Gone now."

I wanted to say that I knew. I wanted him to say it was okay. But he just said, "Don't pull it out so harsh. They don't like that. Let's check on your dad." And he turned to the east.

Dad was on the other side of the flat, 300 yards distant. A silhouette, leaning forward, stalking, just cap and fly rod. Then he stopped moving and began to cast. Three silk strokes, then a release. Crouched now, stripping. We could see the silver explosion, and then the rod bend and him walking into the fish as he reeled. Fight over, he quickly paused and bent, just for a count that I knew was long enough to marvel at its beauty, then release it. He stood straight and looked not to us but to the very blue sky above as a witness.

CHAPTER 3

IT WAS TIME FOR LUNCH on the next flat—a cooler of cold cuts, Bahamian bread, apples, and cheese. We made our own sandwiches and ate off the seats and our laps and paper towels. Dad had a Kalik, and Sebastian and I had little bottled Cokes that were very cold from the icy bottom of the cooler. I was hungry and did not think about anything but how good the food tasted and how blue and bright the sky and water were around us.

We only talked a little between bites, with long pauses of quiet to look at the flats and the distant, low green lines of the surrounding cays.

In the afternoon, the wind picked up, and clouds passed overhead. Sebastian and I walked a flat we called "Anchor" because, at its distant end, a huge, rusted ship's anchor jutted out of the water at low tide. Dad had fallen behind, perhaps with intention, chasing fish he thought he saw. Sebastian stopped still, peering ahead.

"Right here, two o'clock, moving this way. You see them?" The water had only the metal color of the clouds. I saw nothing.

"They there. Thirty feet. Two o'clock. Cast now."

I put the line out and pulled it back, hard against the wind, I felt. The line did not sing but skittered behind me. I brought it forward, then back. I felt the sting of a bee on my backside, knowing from experience that it was a fly hitting me from behind at high speed. I yanked and felt the fly pull at my pants. The line was tangled on the rod tip. I reached my hand back and found the fly stuck fast to my pants. I was a mess.

"Fish gone." He shook his head just a little.

Dad walked up now.

"Tangled up?" he said and smiled. But I did not. I was pulling and tugging at the line and the fly. I would have used a bad word if Sebastian were not there. But I thought it. He was untangling the line from the rod tip. It was a rat's nest.

"Not so hard in the wind."

"I hate the wind."

"It's part of fishing. Wind going to blow; got to learn to fish in it."

"Maybe a little casting practice, Kit." Dad was trying to help. But casting practice was not a happy thought.

It was our backyard at home, Dad methodically counting *one* . . . *two* . . . *three* with me and my brothers. Lines tangled, Mom watching, occasional tears. I knew how to cast. I caught three fish before the wind started blowing. But Dad said, "Sebastian's a better teacher. Why don't you have a try with him?"

So, at our next flat, Sebastian led me to a little split of sand and green on the edge. The seabirds screamed protest at our approach. We set up on the end of the little island, wind quartering to my back. "We going to cast to that branch." His accent made it sound like "*bronch.*" It was a wood snag thirty feet off the beach. He had his fly rod. He let out line and swung the rod. "Look now. Big loop in back, slow. Then out." He released it, and it sang through the air, the end of the line coming to rest inches from the branch.

"Smooth" was his last instruction. This and all the rest were words I knew from my dad, and from him. I stepped up, let out line, and swung the rod. I felt the line knock down behind me in the wind.

"Slow, high. Try again."

I did. And it was worse.

Sebastian demonstrated again, but with new words. "Behind you, beside you, in front."

In a three-count.

I tried, and it was better. But still short, and a little puddly. A few minutes more and he said, "Let's fish now. You ready."

He wanted to fish, not waste time. He gave up. He didn't say it, but I knew it.

The clouds were gone, and the afternoon sun was high and brilliant white. The last flat of the day was so wide that, at the distant end, sea and sky were as one. We walked toward that infinite end. Stalking, casting, missing, catching, smiling. And for me, untangling.

I was very tired when we turned back to the boat, now just a dark spot on the horizon. We walked faster, together, knowing that the wind in our face would thwart us if we saw fish. As at lunch, we spoke little, with grunts and silences. Dad recounted his four fish caught on the flat, and his three bad misses. Dad had put on his wide white hat for the afternoon sun, and his face was smeared with zinc. He'd look silly on land, but here, he was all bonefisherman. He was calm in the telling, teasing himself at a poor cast or a bad strip that lost a fish.

I had caught but had many more misses and did not recount my stories. But Sebastian did.

"Two nice casts. They not feeding." I flinched at only two, but then knew he was right. I'd missed a lot.

Dad summed up as he always did. "A very good day."

The run back was fast, the sun setting in the west behind us. We ran through the dark passes, boat sliding and skimming, then a shortcut over a spot at low tide, Sebastian warning,

"Hold on now."

Dad's arm was around me as the skeg of the engine dragged and caught and skipped in the sand beneath us, and the engine roared, and the boat shuddered, then shot over the shallow flat. Dad gave me a conspiratorial smile through his zinc war paint. I knew he thought the flat was no challenge, and that Sebastian liked to be dramatic with his warnings for the benefit of us children. Dad said, "He's never once been hard aground. I don't think tonight's the night." I hoped not. I was tired and nodding off as the light went away and we approached the cay.

CHAPTER 4

IT WAS A SPIT of sand and rock and tall royal palms, not more than a couple of football fields long, and half as wide. It sat inside the main reef, less than a quarter mile off Money Point, and thus was known as Money Cay.

Dad bought it without telling my mom first. He thought she would be surprised. She said that yes, she was very surprised. It took him two years, without her help, to run power out to the island and build the house. A simple Bahamian cottage, surrounded by a broad veranda. The cost of the house apparently exhausted Dad's extra cash during those years. So Mom took to calling it "No Money Cay." This did not seem funny to Dad. So he stopped calling it Money Cay. He just referred to it as "the cay."

When people at home heard he'd been in the Bahamas, they'd naturally ask which island. He'd be there, at a cocktail party or a reception at the club, surrounded by suits and taffeta, his face slightly burned from sun and wind. He'd say, "A small cay off Andros." They'd dutifully ask which one.

At first, he tried to call it by name, leaving them twisting in their ignorance. But their confusion and repeated questions eventually led to him keeping it very simple. When asked which island, he just said, "The one just south of paradise." They weren't sure if he was serious, and I think he very much enjoyed that.

Veronica was there on the porch when we got back. She cooed and laughed her great laugh and gave me an enveloping hug.

"Look at our girl!" She held me out. "I can see how beautiful you are even in these fishing clothes! Now, is it Kit or Catherine?"

It was definitely Catherine, but for her I said, "Either."

"Well, I think it's Catherine. You can go clean up before your dad uses all the hot water. If he even showers now, staying out here all alone!"

Dad laughed as he came up with the rods and the bag. "I do shower. At least once a week. And when your mother comes."

Veronica had made my favorite—barbecued chicken and peas and rice. I was famished from walking all day in the sun and ate until I was very full, but I didn't care. Dad raised his glass of wine to my Coke and clinked. "To a very good day. Clear eyes and steady hands." It was his favorite toast.

I knew then that I was fully on the cay, and the kitchen glowed as Dad and I cleaned up. We heard Sebastian's skiff cough to life, and he and Veronica buzzed away in the dark to the dock.

I tried to read in bed, but my eyes were heavy, and I settled into the cool sheets, smelling Dad's cigar from the veranda and hearing the whoosh of the ocean over the inner reef. As I closed my eyes and drifted off, I saw the sun dapples of brown, green, and white, and the silver of the flat, and the shadow and flash of fish.

CHAPTER 5

I WOKE TO LOUD YELLING OUTSIDE. For a moment, I thought I was home, that it was my brothers. It was barely light, and I realized I was on the cay. I heard my dad yell from the veranda.

"I'm coming down."

I came out and saw a skiff bobbing at the dock, three Bahamians gesturing wildly, and my dad running down the path. Then they were carrying what looked like a brown, green, and white sack between them. And it was dripping red as they crossed the veranda.

"Bring him to the kitchen."

Dad had cleared the old wood table and spread beach towels over it.

They laid him there, and I saw his calf was torn from the bone, and red flesh and blood pushed out from a flap. He was screaming. The men who carried him were all talking at once, their Andros accents so strong with excitement that I could not understand them. Their eyes rolled back in their heads. My knees felt weak, and the room started to turn over.

"Kit, go get my bag. It's in the closet in my room." I didn't move. I was in my pajamas.

"Kit, now." It was not loud. He looked at me over the man's wound with just the hint of a firm smile.

I ran into his room. I knew the bag. It was a faded red-and-yellow sailcloth satchel Dad had made by the ladies of Man-O-War Cay in Abaco many years before. The bag had been present for stitching up a handful of neighbor kids at home in summers past and for the reattachment of my brother Charlie's earlobe after a backyard football skirmish. It felt heavy, but as I carried it into the kitchen, I did not think there could be enough in it to make the man right again.

Dad had more towels out, and the men were quiet now, watching wide eyed, half turning away. There was so much blood—it was puddling on the floor.

"Fishing accident. Over in Lowe Sound at the pier. Prop went off while he was pushing the boat in the shallows. Lucky he didn't sever his foot. Somebody had the good sense to belt it for a tourniquet." He was talking to me as he prepared a syringe and injected it.

"Hold him still now," he told the men holding the man and his leg. He injected the syringe and then threw it into the sink.

"You're going to be okay. That will help the pain." He was over the man's face now. "Steady. You're going to be okay."

The man moaned through clenched teeth, then a firm nod with his eyes tightly closed, resigned: *Fix me.*

Dad had washed his hands and put on surgical gloves; then he was squirting saline into the wound and daubing it with big gauze pads. He was talking to me again.

"Okay, pretty clean. Salt water helps. Nicked an artery. That's all the blood. Come here."

He was talking to me. He looked at me like he was asking me to go get something for him from the garage at home.

"I've got to stitch this shut. I need your help. Go wash your hands."

I did not see how I could help. Or what could be done. So much blood. The room was turning over again. I got very close to Dad and said quietly, only to him, "Is he going to die?"

He sort of snorted with just a little turnup at the corners of his mouth. "Well, yeah." Then he paused and looked squarely at me, serious now, his eyes very blue and steady. "But not today. Now go wash your hands. Lots of hot water and soap."

And I did. He laid out sutures, surgical instruments, clamps, scissors, and a lot more gauze. He had me put on a clean pair of surgical gloves and told me to hand things to him as he asked, to hold and daub the gauze, to squirt the saline. I watched him work steadily, quickly, but he never rushed. His fine long fingers threaded the suture, holding it up to the light. Then he went to work, holding the wound in one hand and sewing with deft, steady strokes. He daubed more gauze and called for more.

"You with me, Reynolds?" He put his fingers on the man's throat for a moment and looked at his watch.

The man nodded.

"Good. Almost there. You're doing good."

At some point, Sebastian and Veronica had arrived. I heard her and looked up. She was in the doorway. "Oh my! Oh, Reynolds!" She knew the men. "You okay now. Doctor got you."

Sebastian just stood in the doorway, watching gravely beneath his cap.

Dad finished stitching, then went to the man's throat again and felt for a moment.

"You're doing good, Reynolds. We'll get you all wrapped up."

He wrapped the wound tightly in gauze bandages, and then looked at the men.

"Let's get him to the airport. He needs to get to Nassau."

"We already called the plane. They're waiting."

"Good. Keep it high now while we carry him."

He looked at me, "No fishing today, miss. Good job. Thanks for your help. I'm going to get him on the plane. Hold down the fort."

They put him in our skiff and headed to shore, Dad holding the man's hand. He was close to him, and it was hard to tell if he was taking his pulse or comforting him.

Veronica was mopping, and I helped her clean. The blood was like fish blood now and lost its horror. She was quietly singing a low Andros song. When I asked, she told me what it was about as we worked: a fisherman lost at sea for many months, who comes back to his wife after she has given up hope and built a tomb for him. They break up the tomb and use the stones to build the foundation for a new house. I told her I liked the song.

When we finished, the kitchen looked as it had before. She cut up some fruit and made some eggs, but I wasn't very hungry.

Dad and Sebastian returned. Dad gave me a big hug.

"He's going to be okay. Pretty exciting morning, huh? And Mom says the cay is boring!"

I laughed and nodded. I was suddenly ready to cry, even though I believed him when he said the man would be okay.

"Hey. It's okay. It's a lot."

He gave me a bigger hug and a big pat on the back. He held me at arm's length and smiled. "You're practically ready for trauma duty at Broward Memorial!"

I laughed and wiped the tears away.

"You were very steady. Great job. It's going to make you a better fly caster."

This seemed unlikely, but I nodded.

CHAPTER 6

THE CAY WAS OFTEN QUIET. The whoosh of the ocean over the distant reef, the sea breeze ruffling the tall palms. Dad liked to have Nassau radio on low when he was in the workshop. And Veronica liked it on when she was in the kitchen.

Dad liked to play his music. This was, I now realize, a radically eclectic collection of just what he liked. He had Coltrane CDs. He had Muddy Waters and Johnny Cash. There was Brahms and Mozart. And what he proclaimed to be the finest collection of classic old reggae outside of a Kingston record shop.

You'd come up from the dock and hear the Royals or the Melodians moaning on, or a young Bob Marley and his early Whalers echoing from the house. If he was reading or writing or working, he liked quiet. But on these occasions, you'd find him on the veranda in his big chair, smoking a cigar, perhaps tinkering with a reel or a leader. Or slowly pacing the broad porch, bare feet on worn wood, messing around, and very happy.

His writing was also eclectic. He wrote academic pieces for surgical journals on preventing sepsis and cutting angles for internal organ repair.

He wrote pieces about bonefish feeding and hatcheries, and moon cycles for conservation and fishing magazines.

And he wrote poems.

He said that he'd wanted to write fiction as a medical student and resident, but he had little time. Even if he could make the time, he said he had no mental space to create. So he just jotted notes of what he observed. Families in the hospital canteen. His fellow residents. The din of the emergency ward. The quiet of the very early morning hours. Coming home to find my mother waiting up, tired but exquisite.

He shared some of these jottings with his good friend Michael, who wrote for the Baltimore paper. Michael told him that these observations were poetry. He disbelieved it. But Michael insisted. With a bit of editing and shaping, the observations were poems. Michael suggested he read a book on poetry, and some Billy Collins. He realized Michael was not wrong. Poems could be simple, unrhyming, and made up of everyday stuff like hospitals and suburban kitchens.

He began a lifetime habit of jotting these things in a small leather notebook. On occasion, he'd be found bent over it, at early-morning coffee when we came out sleepy in our pajamas at the kitchen table. He might be in his bathrobe, or still in his scrubs from a late night on call. When I was small, I'd climb in his lap and ask what the book was about. He'd always say it was just his scribbling.

Once in a great while, he'd write one for someone, a dear friend or relation. A birthday. An anniversary. A toast. But otherwise, he never read them aloud. He published dozens of articles on surgery and bonefish. But not a single poem.

They were just for him.

CHAPTER 7

THAT AFTERNOON WAS QUIET, and we read and played dominoes. The phone rang midafternoon, and I watched as he talked with the doctor from Nassau.

"Yes, well, good. Just lots of antibiotics, and a close eye on it. Obviously not as clean as we'd like. Okay, yeah. Thanks. Please keep me posted." He hung up and turned to me.

"He's doing fine. Wanted ice cream." He smiled. "How about some casting practice? Try your steady hand."

It did not sound like fun, but I knew he needed distraction.

"Sure, but you said Sebastian is a better teacher, and he gave me a D-plus and sent me away."

"Not true. He said you were doing great."

I knew this was not true because Sebastian never used the word *great* about anything.

We walked to the flat sand and rock at the end of the cay. He turned to me. "Okay, Kit. Clear eyes, steady hand."

"I thought that was for this morning."

"No. That's for everything."

He was looking out at the sea now, and then he turned back to me.

"You have it now. Let's see it."

"Surgery or fly-fishing?"

"What's the difference? See clearly. Work steady. In all things."

I put the line out and began to swing it back and forth.

He looked at me. "No counting now. You're past that. Feel it."

He'd never *not* counted. Not with me or my brothers. The counting was a core of the lesson.

"Feel the line. It's just energy, you know. That's what makes it go. Feel it building in the back."

And then I could. The tension, the build in the line itself. I released it. No, it puddled in front of me.

"Trust it. Don't fling it. Just let it go. Try again."

I did.

"Not too many false casts. You lose it there. Let it go before you think you're ready. When."

It was oddly not a question. I looked at him quizzically. But he just looked out in front of us, at the target for my next cast. Then he repeated, "Before you're ready. When."

Then I felt the line for the very first time. I heard it singing. It tugged through my fingers and hand to my core. I let it go one cast before. That's the only thing I can call that time—*before*.

It shot out fifty feet, straight and true.

"That's very good! You've got it." He laughed.

I laughed back. "Really? That's it?"

"Yeah. That's it."

He raised his eyebrows and smiled. He was sharing one of his secrets. Telling me something that he knew I could now understand.

"Feel it in the line. What was, what is, what will be. No counting, just feeling, knowing when."

I threw more and found the line going to the spot I imagined. He smiled and walked back up to the house. I stayed and practiced, delighting in the feel, the singing of the line on its cast, and my ability to will it to its target.

The next day, I caught eleven fish. All on my own casts. I hit spots far and close. My misses were only from being unaware of how far I could throw, how close the fish were, and how little line I needed to reach them. On the few occasions of a poor cast, I took a breath and thought of the feel of the line. *Was, is, will be.* And it was gone, straight to where I willed it.

When I returned to the skiff after stalking the last flat with considerable success, Dad and Sebastian were waiting at the boat. They clapped. I took a small bow, laughing and splashing with my rod. Sebastian was very happy.

"I think she's got it, Doc."

Dad smiled broadly out of his zinc-smeared face. "Yes, she does, Sebastian. She definitely does."

He lifted his Kalik to toast me and smiled his happiest smile.

CHAPTER 8

JUST WHEN THE FISHING got very good, the weather turned, and the next day, thunderstorms blew us off the flats. The sky was gunpowder gray, and the thunderheads rolled in from the northeast in towering black trains.

I read and drew. Dad turned on some Hopeton Lewis. We sat at the dining room table with the big light on, and he made sure I could tie a blood knot. He showed me what he called the Andros six. His long fingers worked on the line just as they had on the sutures. Steady, strong, and deft. After a while, I could do it on my own. He said it was the very best knot, and one he had never seen until Sebastian taught him the first time they fished together. He went through his box of favorite flies, talking about their advantages and the kind of water and bottom where they worked best.

He dug out some watercolors and asked me to put palette on my sketch of Fish Cay. We decided I'd need another try, though it was a good start. We checked the boat, bobbing and straining at its lines at the dock with each howling band. Dad grilled some crawfish, and we ate the peas and rice Veronica had left before the weather. We decided that, in such conditions, no green vegetables were needed.

That night, I slept and woke only briefly to the howling wind outside, pulling and tugging on the house. I settled back into the cool sheets, feeling steady inside the house on the rock.

In the morning, Dad listened to the Nassau weather and to NOAA from Miami. He squinted to the north and said he could see the tail of it. We would have one more day of fishing after the weather passed. He believed it could be exceptional after a big blow, the fish hungry and reckless.

It was just as he predicted. The fish came across the flats in waves, pushing water, tails glinting in the morning sun. I cast to flight after flight, and watched pairs and threes turn hard like pointers on scent to the fly, tails tipping, hungrily grubbing into the sand. I felt the splendid tugging and jolt, saw the silver eruption, and then heard the reel singing with the breathless run out.

Sebastian laughed and clapped. "Another big one!"

My dad raised his fly rod in salute from the other side of the flat. The sun arched across the sky, blue and high. An airplane buzzed lonely above, headed for Nassau.

Late in the day, Sebastian said I could see the fish myself now, and my dad needed him more. I knew this was not true, but I appreciated him saying it. I was trusted to fish alone.

The sun and light wind were behind, and the flat was lit gold and deep blue. The fish were feeding into the outgoing tide, and I watched them come on, dark formations of sixes and eights pushing the water. I heard the line singing and saw the splash and rip of water.

Sebastian and Dad were far across the flat, figures moving slowly east. Sebastian leaned forward, his hand behind his back, then pointed his long arm forward. Dad casting now, smoothly. A fish fought cleanly and quickly. After the fish, I saw them talking. Dad had to be laughing, bent over, and then he splashed his hands clean and stood straight. He swept his arm, and Sebastian looked that way too, toward the lowering sun and distant cloud fragments tinging from orange to pink.

It was Sunday. Dad never missed Mass at home, but the nearest Catholic parish on Andros was at Fresh Creek, a two-hour drive on potholed roads. He would not take advantage of a travel exemption in a place that he thought of as home. But the difficult trip caused him to have a personal rule. He allowed a miss if he had one of us on the cay to fish and the weather was good. He said that on such days, there could be no grander cathedral than the flats to the north of the cay. So vast as to make real the infinite God and all He wrought.

To make abundantly clear how small we are, and how singularly we are loved.

It was fully manifest to a fourteen-year-old girl on that afternoon. Sea and sky. Wind and tide. Loving and loved.

CHAPTER 9

I RETURNED TO MY LIFE at home somehow changed. My mother's persistent questions and unsolicited advice did not spark a rise of voice or slammed doors. I could simply respond. I could proceed with quiet if I felt myself unspooling. She did not like the quiet, but this new way could get us settled back down again in minutes, not days.

My brothers were slow to see a difference. But they must have felt the change in the house, perhaps not knowing what had brought some peace. When Dad returned a few days after me, they had to listen to his tales of my casting prowess. They did not believe it. They wanted to object. I just smiled and said nothing. They could not call Dad an exaggerator. They had to accept it. I was a skilled angler. That's what he called me. I felt it was true.

I tried to carry this same feeling into my friendships. Monica was full of juicy gossip and details about the time I had been away. I listened and felt a rise of anger as I heard Barbara Pennington's reported slight about me. But I thought of Barbara, with her slouch and over-teased hair, holding forth in a group reveling in the brief attention. The rise was replaced with a sadness for her. Monica wanted more from me than to hear that it was too bad. When she pressed, I change the subject.

She did not want to hear about my time on the cay. Or anything else. She wanted to talk, and I was willing to listen. But she left the house thinking I was moody and disinterested. I told her I was neither. But I probably was the latter.

I drew and painted. I still wasn't very good, but it felt good to put the pencils and brushes on the canvas, to see their marks. I read my summer reading in a rush. I probably did not give Camus his due.

The remaining weeks before school were a flurry of shopping for books and backpacks and clothes. This would have been a time that I could not abide my mother and her dictates on uniform purchases, clothing styles, and the right type and amount of makeup for a girl my age. But I listened. I asked questions about *why*. She gave me answers, albeit impatiently. I gave in on most of her demands after talking but won a few small concessions after explaining myself.

The halls of Our Lady of Mount Carmel Academy would present the greatest challenge. It was here, amid the stew of teenage-girl cynicism and angst, that I had found my bluest and most irritable self. I had marked myself out the prior year as someone who challenged teachers on sometimes trivial points, and one who was not afraid to push the edges of rules that seemed poorly thought out and administered.

Sister Mary Veronica did not disappoint my expectations. She smiled at me carefully as I walked through the entry portico on the first day. She greeted me and asked me how my summer had been.

I gave her a smile, the first in quite some time, and told her it had been wonderful, but I was glad to be back. I thought this small white lie was worth it to try to reset the scales for what I hoped would be a happier year.

But she and the faculty were, if anything, more autocratic than the year before. There were arbitrary uniform demands and exorbitant penalties for shoes that weren't brown enough or not polished sufficiently. Makeup was wiped from the faces of classmates. These things would have sent me into rebellious sulks before. But now I saw them as the way things were—the reality of my days. I could accept it. This resolve meant I could look ahead and not thrash against these rulings and their injustice.

I made honor roll the first quarter and, just as importantly, chalked up only one demerit. This was a double coup in my record at the school that I had not achieved previously. My dad and mom noticed. Privileges were granted. I was able to stay up thirty minutes later on weeknights, and until midnight on Friday and Saturday. They offered to let me host a sleepover, but I couldn't think of anyone I wanted to spend that much time with.

In the second quarter, two of my drawings were chosen for display outside the chapel, where the artwork from previous year's winners hung. I used colored pencils, and one sketch was of the view from the cay. Girls asked me where it was. I told them it was *the one just south of paradise.*

In early spring, I was rushing down a hallway from the studio to my next class when I nearly ran into Sister Mary Veronica. She actually laughed when I nearly dropped my books. It was, I think, the first time I had seen her really smile. "Oh, Catherine, you're in a rush! I've been meaning to talk with you. Will you be putting your name in for leadership next year?"

One thing I liked about Sister was that she never called me Kit. And she pronounced Catherine very nicely. It took me a moment to appreciate those things, and to understand what she meant by leadership. I must have paused too long because she added, "Student government? An officer for your class?"

I stuttered, "Well, no, I hadn't really given it any thought, Sister."

"Well, you should. I think you'd be very good."

I nodded.

"Get along to class. You don't want Mrs. Fuller to miss you."

I rushed to class, wondering what Sister had possibly seen that would make her think I could serve as a class officer, or even compete in an election for such a spot.

But when I floated the idea at lunch, no one laughed, and no one seemed shocked at all. Linda Cabrera said I'd be great. She warmed to the idea of my being a staunch advocate for sensible and much-needed uniform changes. Monica took a swipe at the presumptive class president, Katie Sabelus, but I ignored that and took her comment as support for the idea.

Mom was visibly stunned when I told her that night. She quickly recovered and told me she thought it was a great idea. But she also spent a fair amount of time over the next few days saying that running for office was the real experience, and I shouldn't get my hopes up. This rankled me.

Dad gave it his usual. "That sounds great. I think you'd be terrific. Go for it." He'd have probably said the same thing if I had told them I was pursuing lion taming, but I liked his approach better, even though he obviously knew next to nothing about all-girls Catholic school student government politics.

By the middle of April, I had put my paints and brushes to work on poster board and created colors and a logo I really liked. Consistent with its claustrophobic rules, the school would only allow us to put campaign signs in three set places on the entire campus. So the colorful poster board was a narrow but important shot at recognition. With ninety girls in the class, I couldn't hope to talk to them all. I regretted not having a wider circle of friends. I fretted over my speech to the class. I had decided to run for vice president and avoid a frontal confrontation with Katie. But there was a set slate of longtime student government groupies. I was a dark horse, and no one needed to tell me that.

The speech was risky. Instead of going on about the usual policy points of changes in the lunchroom and uniform rules, I decided to talk about service. To one another. To the community outside the gates of the school. It was very quiet in the chapel when I rose to speak. It got quieter as I covered my subject, and I thought I was bombing. But to my surprise, there was very loud applause when I finished, and lots of smiles and squeezes of the arm as I made my way through the girls afterward. I heard "great speech" muttered as I passed.

I won by two votes. My vanquished opponent, Angela Ricci, would not forgive me until senior year. Even then, I think she may have held a grudge. I had upset the political landscape of our little school. I couldn't believe I'd been bold enough to run for office, giving a speech on something so unpopular. I was stunned that I won.

The last day of school, Sister Mary Veronica stopped me as I was carrying out a box of things from my locker.

"Catherine, so pleased at all you have accomplished this year. What a difference a year makes."

For the first time—but not the last—I could only agree with her.

CHAPTER 10

MY BROTHERS DID NOT have to go to the cay to find my father. They could find him at the hospital, on his rounds, in his white pressed coat, hurrying from floor to floor, clipboard in hand, scribbling orders in his scrubs, and then having a quick cup of coffee and a bowl of soup in the cafeteria. They could look him in the eye there and chat about metastatic pressure or the use of cortisone. There was a new common language for them now. My brothers, who had followed their father into medicine—better, into surgery.

So, around the dinner table on a Sunday or over a rum on the porch, Charlie, newly finished with a fellowship at Dad's old program, could talk with some authority about his curious and difficult cases while Dad smiled and peered into his glass, nodding. And Kevin, in the midst of his own fellowship at UM, could observe insurance frustrations and overwork fatigue. And Dad could tell stories about how it used to be. I'd sit quietly, waiting for the talk to turn to art or fly-fishing. I'd often end up in the kitchen with Mom, cleaning up.

Our shared exile from the surgical ward brought us together. After all these years, she might have known as much about surgery as a first-year resident, but she hardly ever participated. It felt to me like she had tired of tissue stents and falling blood pressure.

She was fifty-four that year, and we three children had grown her out of her job. The house itself had become a focus for her fierce energy. A renovation of the bathrooms and guestroom had been followed by a large and intricate landscape project. She played tennis three times a week. She read widely and voraciously. She wanted to travel more.

I looked at her back bent over the sink. Slim as a girl, dark hair pulled back over a Lily blouse. Only when she turned to ask me for a platter did I see the crow marks of age and sun on her high cheeks and around her bright-green eyes. I could only think that I would like to look like her in thirty years.

She was asking me about Drew. He was one subject that she returned to often that year. The other was my job. Or what was passing for a job.

Drew and my not-really-job were similar. I had Drew, and I had my job as a graphic designer for a Miami ad agency—but I wasn't really sure I wanted either of them. But I knew I *should* want both. My mother was clear on this each time the two subjects came up.

"He's not going to hang around forever. And it's not fair to him after nearly a year."

I looked at my wineglass and thought about that. Both statements were true. I nodded. She leaned back on the counter, drying her hands. They were tan and veined, and the diamond she wore hung largely on her thin fingers.

"I'm not trying to push you, but you need to think about it. You need to be fair to him."

"I know." My quiet did not work with my mom. She'd been trained by Dad. She'd push on.

"He's a good guy. Successful. You like him. He's good looking. He's crazy about you."

Dad was in the kitchen doorway now.

"Drew? Are we on Drew again?" He was smiling and rinsing his dessert plate in the sink. He turned to us. "He doesn't fish."

"He does fish, Dad."

"Casting dead shrimp is not fishing."

"Don't be a snob, Jack," Mom interjected.

"I'm not a snob. He lacks patience. That's what I'm talking about."

"There are other qualities for Catherine to consider besides fishing."

"Are there?" He looked at me, then at Mom. He laughed. But I wasn't sure he was joking. He may not have been sure either.

I knew that, for him, fishing was not about the sport. It was a test of necessary virtues.

Patience.

Quiet.

Persistence.

Grace.

Appreciation for beauty.

And of forces larger than yourself.

Being fully present.

HE DID NOT CARE if people fished badly, so long as they sincerely tried. I knew this because I'd made the mistake of bringing two roommates to the cay for spring break my sophomore year in college. Neither fished, but they jumped at the chance to join me as a guest on my "private island in the Bahamas."

Sometimes, on the potholed drive from the airport in Dad's beat-up Suburban, I realized I'd badly oversold this. Looking out at unfinished, weathered houses and stands of ragged Andros pine, I could see they knew they were a long way from the Caribbean resort they had envisioned. I'm not sure who regretted it the most—me, the girls, my dad, or Sebastian.

Probably Sebastian.

But the girls were game. They were good sports. And Dad appreciated their spirit and effort.

He was patient. More patient than Sebastian, who growled and sulked at the horrific casting, the tangled lines, and females clucking and giggling in the skiff when he was quietly scanning the flats to find fish for us.

Dad took it as a challenge and seemed to ignore or miss the lack of legitimate interest. He let us have a few Kaliks, though we were only nineteen. He said Bahamian law applied. The girls thought he was funny and charming with his battered oxford shirt and sunburnt face.

They were even more charmed with Mom when she arrived midweek with a cooler full of good wine and artisan cheese. She arrived looking tan and fit in her sundress and straw hat. She gave voice to what they had only thought.

"Jack, this room looks like New American fishing shack. Where are the pillows I brought?"

Mom scanned the room with a furrowed brow. She turned to my friends. "Sorry, girls. Whenever I'm not here for more than a few days, this place goes from island home to fish camp."

She went right to the closet and found the toile pillows she'd brought over the year before and placed them on the couch and big chairs. Dad just looked bemused. He carried her bags into their room.

At dinner, she had some wine and told several amusing stories. Dad and I had heard them, or lived them, but the girls found them hilarious. They loved the "No Money Cay" story.

Dad and I did the dishes, and I could hear her holding forth. They were asking where she bought her sundress, and about her nails and pedicure.

In the remaining days of our visit, their interest in fishing went from mild to none. It meant I couldn't fish either. Mom took us to Nicholls Town to buy Androsian fabrics, and to Red Bays for straw bags and hats. On the flight back to Virginia, they raved about my dad and mom, but mostly Mom.

The next spring break came and went, and they did not ask to go back. I did not invite guests to the island in the years that followed.

My one serious college boyfriend did not get an invite. I think he would have gone. He was from Main Line, Philadelphia, and I could not imagine him fishing, or even on the cay. He mocked his own lack of physical activity. I liked the fact that he mocked it, but I also realized how different it made us.

I was an infrequent visitor to the cay in those college years. I was so very busy. I went abroad to Italy. I worked very hard in school. I went to the cay for special occasions. Dad's fiftieth birthday. Easter twice. No long visits.

Then, in that first year after college, I found myself with time. I read books I wanted to read. The college boyfriend was off to MBA school up north. I lived in an apartment in Miami alone. And the cay became important again.

I could hop a cheap flight over on Friday afternoon and be there by sunset. Dad was there often, sometimes Mom too. But other times, it was just me. Sebastian and Veronica would get me settled and checked in. And then I had the broad, sunlit veranda, the reef, and the cool wood floors all to myself. I read, tried to paint, slept, and drank cold wine.

And I fished.

Sebastian would take me far up into the Joulter Cays, to the big flats at the very northern edge. We would fish quietly and steadily. He still had much to teach me, but it might only be a single short lesson in a day of fishing—the way the fish fed into or with a tide, depending on the depth of the flat, or how the fly should be placed for a single fish moving quickly. He said I knew a lot, but we agreed there is always more to learn.

Mom had always complained that there was no bathtub on the cay. Dad said there was a good reason for that. Our water came from rain caught off the roof, into gutters, then piped into the cistern beneath the house. It was limited, and a shower used a fraction of what a tub consumed.

Mom maintained that baths were a sign of civilization. Ultimately, Dad relented, but in his own way. He brought a huge, galvanized tub from Miami and rigged an outdoor bath in a wooden enclosure. The rainwater heated all day in a tank above the tub, and a pull on the lanyard filled the tub with pure, beautiful, and hot rainwater. Bone tired and salty after walking the flats, I luxuriated in that tub, looking up at the palm branches in the late blue darkness of the remaining day above.

I would return to my job on Monday feeling light and steady, patient with the chaos and politics of the agency, with new energy for yet another iteration of the logo for a new pool cleaning product.

My job was a *job*. It seemed like drudgery. Dad said that's why they call it a job. But I knew he had more to say than that heavy pessimism. He did not have a job. He had medicine. Over the years, in unguarded moments, I had heard him ruthlessly pity those stuck in a mere job, without a vocation.

"Working for the weekend," he'd chortle. "Spending five days of your life so you can have two days you like. That's not a life."

He was too kind to tell his daughter that was exactly what she was doing. But I knew that he knew. The closest he would come to the truth would be occasionally asking me if I was painting. Whatever I might say in response to that question, I was not painting. There were canvases stacked in the spare room of my apartment. Some even had paint on them. But if I was honest, I was not painting.

It was hard to say why not. If pressed, I'd say, "There's just no time." But there were plenty of idle hours for books or sleep or talking to friends or watching *Seinfeld*. It wasn't a lack of time. It was what my dad called mental space. He said it was why he couldn't write fiction as a young doctor. You might carve out the time, but your mind (and he might add soul) were not sufficiently present. Too preoccupied with the push and shove of the day to create.

I felt that now when I tried to paint. I could mix the paints and hold the brush. But when I raised my hand to the canvas, I felt nothing. Mechanical lines would follow. The canvas and my hand were not alive.

So I'd walk away. For coffee. To sit on my balcony. To go for a run. To make a phone call. A Saturday set aside to paint often produced nothing—not a single clean line I loved, no shape that was true.

IN THAT GAP between work and the cay came Drew. My weekends went from guilty and idle artist to frenetic, fun girl. A 5K run on Brickell. An Argentinian food fair on Key Biscayne. An afternoon party at a friend's house in Stiltsville. Dancing in South Beach. Dinner with friends at a Cuban joint we all loved. I played very hard and was exhausted by Sunday evening. There was no time to feel guilty about the blank canvases.

Drew taught me about wine. Not just that it tasted good, but why. He came from a family that knew those things. He had traveled. Not to the Bahamas. To Europe, Asia, South America. Being from Chicago, not Miami, he taught me to see South Florida with fresh eyes. Las Olas had charm. Art Deco didn't look tired when he described it. Heat was good. Knowing Spanish mattered. His was weak, but he was learning.

That might have been the only thing, in those days, where I was stronger. My ability to catch phrases in Cuban Spanish, not the kind you learned in school. My casual-conversational grammar picked up after years spent talking with friends in Spanglish. On everything else we were doing together, he was stronger.

Except fishing. He had grown up going to a cabin in Northern Michigan. He knew the basics of spin casting for bass or perch or even a pike. He knew rowboats. His fishing education had stopped in elementary school.

That's what Dad said. I thought that was unfair in many ways. And I fought him on it. I defended an otherwise intelligent and sporty man who thought throwing a plug for fish was fair game. Though I did not believe it myself, I took on the defense of that practice—with the vigor and passion of someone raised in a family full of vigorous and passionate quarreling.

And Drew never knew. He somehow missed the raised eyebrows and smirks of my brothers and my dad when he described getting a snook on a top water plug in a Miami canal. Drew told the story to be "in." And it just put him further out. It was cruel. It made me mad. I defended him because he was weak. There, in his perfect Patagonia fleece, with his finely chiseled nose. Earnest. Handsome. Clueless.

It was hard to forgive.

So, I doubled down. I'd take him to the cay. With my dad. Real fly-fishing. He'd prove he was adaptable. Teachable. Aware. That he had the qualities I wanted: Patience. Discipline. Quiet. A clear eye and a steady hand.

I knew this last would be a challenge. Drew was very athletic. He'd played soccer through high school, and he could run. But his hands and eyes did not really agree.

He couldn't throw. Literally. At a bar with a basketball game, he missed the rim. From eight feet. With a toy ball. Twice. He laughed it off and drank a beer. I winced for him. It didn't matter. But it did.

So, I knew he'd have to practice. How do you tell a twenty-eight-year-old man that you might be in love with that he needs to practice fly-casting in order to pass muster with your family?

You try to be light and funny about it. But he asks you, "Practice? How hard can it be to cast a fishing rod?" in a way that tells you he does not understand, and he will not practice. Unless you insist. At which point, he becomes defensive. And really resists practicing.

I didn't need to practice at this point in my life. But I did anyway, in the hope that he'd see me doing it and want to join in. But he just watched. He drank wine and acted bored after just a few minutes. He actually teased me about missing the target I was casting to but refused to give it a try himself. He did not know what he did not know. Including that it hurt me that he thought what I was doing was easy. Because it wasn't.

He found out how difficult it was three weeks later on the flats. There was a typical ten-knot northeast wind as we set out from the cay early that morning. The day was otherwise perfect, blue skies, sun behind us, and a falling tide.

Drew and I sat on the seat in front of the console, and Dad stood next to Sebastian as he steered the skiff through the dark blue of the winding channels cutting the flats. I looked back at them in the light of the morning sun, alike in all but the color of their battered cotton shirts, ball caps, and sunglasses. Dad had three days of beard. He gave me a nod and a smile. Sebastian kept his eyes straight ahead on the water. They were like a pair of saltwater flats thieves. Drew did not see any of this. He tilted his head back, smiled up at the sky, and squeezed my knee.

At the first flat, Sebastian staked the boat, and we climbed out. We could see a dark mass in the distance with tails flashing silver in the early morning sun. Sebastian nodded toward them and gestured. "We'll go up this way. Drew, you come with me, this side."

Dad and I worked up the left side. Thirty yards to our right, Drew was a few steps behind Sebastian, who was in his typical stalking posture, leaning forward, an arm tucked behind his back, walking slowly.

There were well over 100 fish huddled together. A few small lemon sharks worked around the back edges of the herd. A mass of fish like this was not easy. They may be together but nervous and not feeding. We had to cast to the edges and draw out a fish. A poor cast into the pack could spook them all. Dad and I both knew this, and we did not need to say it to one another.

I glanced over and saw Sebastian gesturing to Drew, no doubt explaining this to him in his hoarse whisper. It also did not need to be said amongst the three of us that we would give Drew the first shot.

He stripped out line, then drew it back twice, then swung his rod forward very hard, just like a spinning rod. The line fell harmlessly at his feet. Sebastian helped him gather the line, and they edged closer to the fish. Drew tried again. The same result. Sebastian was raising his arm over his head, in a broad sweep, back and forth, showing him. I knew the words he was whispering. "Slow now. Not so much line. Then let it go."

It was better, but still very short. I looked at Dad. He was watching also. He said nothing. I could not read his eyes behind the sunglasses. We moved closer, staying even with them. We were less than forty feet from the front edge of the school. It was time to cast while the fish were still there. I did not want to catch a fish before Drew did.

I looked over and saw another flipped puddle of yellow line in the water in front of him. He could not get a line out to the fish.

"Take a shot, Kit." Dad spoke softly to my left.

I shook my head. "Let's wait." He nodded in a way that did not agree.

A bigger shark had turned up and worked slowly and curiously toward Dad. As he approached closer, Dad slapped the water with his rod tip once, then again, and the shark moved away.

Drew and Sebastian were now less than thirty feet from the fish, and the pack became agitated. Drew took another cast and got it closer, but no fish came out to it. Then, suddenly, the pack of fish erupted, all tails and fins thrashing in the water, torpedo shadows flashing away in all directions.

Then they were gone, leaving only a few darting stragglers and a couple of lazily moving sharks.

Sebastian turned back for the boat, walking ahead of Drew. He did not look over at us, but I heard him say, "They gone now."

Dad and I joined up and walked back with Drew.

Dad spoke first. "Nice school of fish. Hard to catch the pack like that."

Drew shook his head. "Yeah, just couldn't get it in there."

"It'll come."

I could only manage a "Yeah."

So went the next two hours. Puddling tangled lines. Spooked fish. After the third flat, Sebastian became even quieter than usual and steered us back to the channel without a word or a glance at any of us.

Drew sat on the console bench, drinking a bottled water.

"This is hard."

I agreed. Dad said nothing.

Sebastian found a flat with little water. Fish could be seen tailing and grubbing into the falling tide.

"We'll just have a few minutes here."

Sebastian knew the tide would soon leave the flat dry, but there were hungry and careless fish, giving Drew the best chance to hook up.

We fished together now, working within fifteen yards or so abreast of each other. Drew laid a limp line out in front of a grubbing pair moving methodically toward it. I heard Sebastian tell him to wait, then he said, "Strip, strip . . . wait . . . strip." The fish tipped up and pounced on the fly, and he was hooked, churning away in a rip of water. Drew yanked the rod up. The line went slack.

"No. You can't horse him. This not a trout, man!" The fish had broken off when Drew pulled the rod up. He slouched and looked down at his feet.

I could not help him, just offering, "Good hook up."

Dad added, "Yeah, good fish."

Then Dad turned away. He was done helping. He was going to fish. He worked away from us across the flat, catching three fish quickly.

I stayed with Sebastian and Drew. They were saying very little to each other now. I was not going to wait any longer either.

I cast at the first three that moved toward us. The lead fish turned on my fly, and his tail tipped up. I strip set, and he was on. I felt the rumbling tear of the line through my fingers and heard it sing in the reel. I landed him, a beautiful six-pound fish. I took him off myself, revived him, and let him go. He swam away quickly. I washed my hands in the salt water and stood up. Drew laughed with appreciation. "You're pretty good at this."

"Yeah, been doing it a while."

Sebastian laughed now for the first time all morning. "I taught her everything she knows."

"That's true." I laughed. "Come on, let's catch some more fish."

We turned into the falling tide.

Sebastian walked beside us, and he was happy now. Drew tried on another set, but the line got badly tangled behind him. He was embarrassed, and I felt for him. Sebastian took the rod on the next fish and cast it for him. The fish refused, but Sebastian did the same a few minutes later and hooked up. He handed the singing rod to Drew and talked him through landing the fish. It was a nice one, and I snapped a picture of Drew with it. He smiled as we congratulated him, and high-fived us. But the guide had caught it for him, and he knew it.

When we returned to the boat, Drew dug into the cooler and grabbed a beer. It was barely ten o'clock, and I raised my eyebrows at him. He smiled as he opened it.

"What? A beer? Fishing and beer. They go together, right? Like peanut butter and jelly?"

I laughed but did not think that was true. We'd always have a few beers in the cooler. We might have one at lunch, and usually one at the end of the day as we headed home. But not midmorning.

At the next flat, he fished for a while without success, then went back to the boat on his own. When we returned, he was having another beer and a sandwich.

"How'd you do?" His mouth was full.

"Pretty good. What happened to you?"

"Oh, just took a break. Figured I'd let Sebastian fish a little."

I didn't say anything. I poked around in the cooler for a granola bar.

"So, you do this all day?"

He was leaning back on the front of the boat.

"Yeah." I took my sunglasses and hat off, and then I shook out my hair. "Why?"

"Well, it's a lot. A lot of walking. The fish are pretty finicky."

"Yeah, they can be."

"What time do you think we'll head back to the house?"

It was a question that had not occurred to me since I was very little.

"At dark, I guess. Unless the weather turns."

Dad and Sebastian were back, and we moved to another flat quietly. We saw few fish there, though we stalked it end to end, the sun getting high and bright, the flat very white.

We had lunch at the next flat. Drew said he might just take a nap as he covered his face with his hat and lay back in the bow of the boat.

Dad looked at me, bemused. Sebastian was walking away already. I just said, "Okay, see you in a bit."

The three of us fished the flat together, and we caught many fish. For a moment, I forgot about the boy in the boat asleep. My shoulders and neck relaxed.

As we walked back, Dad asked, "You think he's having fun?"

"Yeah."

"It's hard to learn."

"Yeah, it is."

"Casting, all of it."

"Yeah. Takes practice."

"Lots of practice." He laughed.

"Yeah, lots."

"Think he's willing to put the work in?"

"Doesn't seem like it." I smiled and looked straight ahead at the boat.

That afternoon, we fished two more big flats, and Drew drank three more beers. His casting did not improve, but with Sebastian's help, he landed another fish. He seemed tired, and he did not have to say that he was ready to go.

When we turned for home, he became hearty again, laughing as he talked about the fish and the flats. He teased himself about his casting futility. At dinner, after quite a bit of wine, he admitted that he should have practiced. He joked that it was a lot of work for a fish you couldn't eat.

When I broke up with him a month later, he was very upset. He thought it had been the fishing.

"Wait, you're breaking up with me because I can't bonefish?"

"No. That's not why we're breaking up."

"Well, forgive me, but it's been totally different with us since our fishing trip."

I hated that phrase "fishing trip," but I let it pass and just looked at his apartment wall. In the face of my silence, he went on.

"I mean, that's ridiculous. You know how ridiculous that is? This crazy fishing thing, you and your family?

"It's not about fishing, okay? We're not clicking here. That's it. I'm sorry."

Because I knew it would not help, I did not try to tell him that it was not fishing—but rather everything else that I loved and he lacked.

I was decisive this one time. It was a skill I was trying to work on. Then there was a gap in my days. Saturdays were quiet. No more 5Ks or festivals. No couples' dinners. Sundays were quieter. I rattled around my little place that seemed bigger now. I watched cable, clicking through the many channels, finding nothing. This all made me sad and made me think I might have been mistaken.

I tried filling the gap in my weeks with wine. I started having more than a glass or two on weeknights. I found quickly that a bottle was not quite enough. I did not like the clink of the empty bottles in the recycling bin in the mornings.

Running and the StairMaster looked like a better filler. I ran a lot. I got very lean. If I missed my run, I felt a flushed panic. I managed to get a stress fracture in my foot that required a boot.

I drank more wine and ate less. My mother said I was too thin and looked tired. I wasn't sure about too thin, but I did feel tired.

Miami was big enough that I had only run into Drew twice. I thought it would be nice on a Thursday night to call him. I was a little drunk, with a catch in my throat. It had been less than four months. We carefully stayed on easy topics, discussing what we were up to and a few mutual friends. He sounded very different, and I felt no comfort in the voice on the phone.

"I'm sorry. I didn't handle things very well."

I hadn't planned to say that. I didn't feel that I needed to apologize. But I wanted to hear his voice soften.

It didn't.

"Nothing to apologize for. It's what people do. It's worked out."

He did not use my name at any point in the conversation. We said we should have coffee. We did not set a time. When I hung up, I knew that was gone.

CHAPTER 12

THEN I LOST MY JOB. Or I had to quit. Or it was mutual. Or I was being let go. It was unclear to me. It even seemed like a good thing.

Two days after it happened, my friend Caroline was trying to comfort me on the phone.

"So, they can't just do that. There is no justification for that."

"Well, it doesn't matter."

"It does matter. They can't fire you without a reason."

"Fire me? They didn't fire me. I quit."

It was quiet.

"Sorry, I thought you said they said it wasn't working out."

"Well, yeah, but I mean, they never said *fired*."

"Okay. Well, whatever. Look, I know this is hard for you."

I hadn't thought it was hard. But now I reconsidered.

"I know it's hard, Catherine, single and unemployed at this point. But it's going to be so good to reset. Lots of good things."

Single and unemployed. Now I felt bad.

I took no further advice from friends.

I had a boot, no job, and no boyfriend.

But on the third day of my unemployment, I walked into the spare room of my apartment with a large mug of coffee, and I began to paint. And I did not stop painting for five days, except for Cuban takeout and occasional sleep.

When I looked around the apartment, I saw empty wine bottles, a stack of unread *Miami Herald* newspapers, and two canvases humming with light. I felt spent and clean. I slept for thirteen hours without waking or even dreaming.

I went to dinner at my parents' that Sunday night. I had not told them about the job. Driving north on I-95, I thought about how I would tell it. I much preferred *quitting*, and thought it was true enough to tell it that way.

Mom greeted me at the door and said I looked tired. Dad came into the hall. He said it was the boot.

"The boot? What does the boot have to do with tired, Jack?" She likely did not expect an answer, but he had one. "Can't run, bad sleep; plus, she's hobbling around. That'll make you seem tired. Ultimately, it's the boot—just an effect, really."

He gave me a hug.

"You look great. How are you?"

I nodded quickly. "Good." And for the first time in quite a while, I meant it.

We sat on the back veranda. Mom and I drank wine, and Dad had a rum. It took a while for them to ask about work.

"I quit. I've started painting."

Dad just looked bemused. Mom reacted. "Quit? Why? How?"

I grabbed a grape from the hors d'oeuvres tray and popped it in my mouth.

"Yeah. Well, it wasn't working out."

"Well, what are you going to do?"

"Paint." I smiled more steadily than I felt.

She looked at Dad as if to say *do something*. He raised his eyebrows and smiled at her, and then at me. He said, "Starving artist! We've always needed one of those. It'll add some color to the family, honey."

"Starving. She's already starving. Look at her. You'll move home, I suppose?"

I had not supposed that. I had not even thought about my apartment on Brickell and its big monthly rent. I had a little in savings.

"I don't know. We'll see how I do."

"Catherine, you're not seriously planning to live on your art? You know how long it takes to get going? To sell enough? What's the plan here?"

This was a phrase of my mother's that I disliked very much. I felt a hot flush on my face. I thought of the two bright canvases in my apartment and wished I had brought them to show her. I rallied.

"No plans right now, Mom. Just planning to eat dinner. I'm starving, remember?" I laughed at my lame joke and got up to refill my glass. Dad got up too and followed me to the kitchen. Mom sat for a while longer, and then joined us in the kitchen. We fixed our plates in silence.

Dinner was quiet. I caught up on Dad's schedule, discussing a trip they planned to take to Europe. It would mean missing weeks of fishing, but he knew Mom wanted the trip very much.

Dad walked me out to my car.

"Mom will be okay. Just give her a little time to absorb this. She's just worried about you."

"I'm going to be fine."

"Yeah, I know. But you do need to think about money a little. Do you have something set aside for this?"

"Sure. I'll be fine." I did not believe this at all and was starting to do figures in my head.

"Well, let me know if you need some help."

"Thanks, Dad."

I got in the car, and he closed the door. I rolled down the window, and he leaned in.

"Hey, I'm proud of you. It's the right thing. But that doesn't mean it won't be hard."

I nodded. He smiled. "Clear eyes, steady hand."

"Yeah." I laughed and squeezed his hand, and then I drove off.

It was hard. My savings were gone by the third month. I gave up the apartment and rented a worn, two-room quadplex in an unfashionable and unimproved edge of Coconut Grove. Even with that, I was quickly reduced to eating beans and rice. I stopped going out.

Dad sent a check without being asked. I was proud, but not too proud to cash it. I bought fresh fruit, flowers, and some wine. It helped that I knew, without asking, that he hadn't told Mom.

When I talked with her, I tried to sound confident. But she'd seen the place near the Grove and knew I was struggling.

"Just try this at home."

I could not imagine that. Painting, no job, single, living at home. But at least the boot was gone. I could not run, but I was walking fiercely.

And I was painting. I had eleven good pieces and two more in process. The work felt urgent, and my hands and arms tingled when I thought of it. I missed it like someone I wanted to be around.

The days passed quickly—flashes of light to dark to light. Then a welcomed and very deep sleep. Coffee was nearly free, and Mom took me to the art supply store in Plantation to stock up on canvas and paints.

A friend from the agency had a friend who had a gallery in the Gables. It was small, still new. It had broad windows and raw concrete floors. The owner, Bernard, was round and cheerful. He would take my best ten. He'd consider an opening. Wine and beer only.

I sold two pieces for $700 at the opening. The others moved slowly in the weeks that followed. The prices were beaten down, just a couple hundred for some.

It was not enough. I'd spent four months—and all my cash. I couldn't make my rent.

I was crying on the phone with my dad. I was twenty-five, embarrassed.

"What about the cay?"

"What about it? I can't fish. I can't even think."

"No, not to fish. Go stay over there for a while and paint. You can live there on very little."

I paused, and we were quiet.

"Catherine? What do you think?"

"I think it would be great. But it's way too much, Dad."

"Too much? It's free."

"No, it's not. It's expensive, and it's your and Mom's place."

"No, no. It's all of ours. I built it for all of us. It's perfect for you at this moment. It would make me very happy to have you use it."

I hung up the phone and looked around the two dingy rooms. The thought of sea and light made me want to drive to the airport immediately, leaving everything but the canvases for someone else to clean up.

CHAPTER 13

MOM WAS OPPOSED to the idea. We both knew she didn't care about me using the house, but she didn't like me being there alone.

"It's not safe, Jack. And what if something happens?"

We sat at the kitchen island, coffee and half-eaten bagels in front of us. Dad was working his way through the Saturday *Sun-Sentinel*. He looked up over his readers propped on the end of his nose.

"What's going to happen, Margaret? I mean, it's on the edge of the world. Sebastian and Veronica will be checking on her. Besides, she's a pretty independent girl." He winked at me and grinned.

Mom wasn't having it. "Jack, you're not being sensible. You keep a gun on the island. Okay? What else do I need to say?"

"That's just a precaution. Never even thought of using it."

"You keep it for a reason. Be honest with yourself, now."

"Okay. And Kit can use it too. If she had to. But she won't have to. That cay is so out of the way. And it's North Andros. She'll be safe. I'm just not worried. She's in more danger in Miami."

I'd never thought of the cay as unsafe. In fair weather, we often slept with the house wide open. I paused on the thought of being alone on the cay. But I'd gone there many weekends, fishing.

"Mom, how many weekends did I go down without you and Dad? You never said anything. I'm fine. I'm a big girl now." I tried to laugh, but she did not.

She was standing now. She crossed her arms, shook her head, and looked down with a frown. "I'm against this. But you two know best."

Dad and I had heard this before. We'd have to weather this front. But she'd be okay. He had the good sense to offer more coffee, and I got busy clearing up the bagels.

Mom had said she would not go down to help me get settled, but then she relented at the last minute. She heard us talking about supplies and what to pack, and she couldn't be silent any longer. "Oh, my goodness, Jack. You'll have her camping out on the dock. This isn't a fishing trip. I'll have to make sure she's settled in."

She added a case of wine, good coffee, better pillows and bedding, and a carton of books from her book club. With a duffel of clothes and boxes of art supplies, we were loaded for my move.

On the cay, she fussed around the house, putting things in their correct spots. She cleaned out the refrigerator and wiped it down. She remade the beds.

Dad and I fished that afternoon, late to catch the incoming tide. Sebastian had a family event, so it was just the two of us. It was the first time I'd been able to walk the flats since the boot came off and my fracture healed. I missed some fish and my foot ached from walking. But as the sun disappeared, the flat turned to gold. and I was glad just to be out there again.

We walked together on one last stalk, working closer to the boat. Singles and doubles moved slowly, feeding with the tide. Dad silently pointed with his rod. There was a pair coming toward me.

I cast, landing the fly just in front of the leading fish. His tail popped up, and I felt the churning tug. He bolted, and the reel cried. Then I heard a splash to my left and saw that dad had a fish on too. We both laughed, fought the fish in together, chattering, talking to the fish, and watching for the sharks.

We landed and released them, pausing only for a moment to look. He smiled as we turned toward the boat. "Good job. You're going to get pretty good living down here."

"I'm painting, not fishing." I wanted him to know I was serious.

"Well, there's time for both. And they're not exclusive, are they?"

I shook my head and smiled.

"I'm not sure. You always say that. I'm not painting fish. Or fishing."

"No, that's not it. The vision. The grace. The perfect stroke. Brush stroke or casting stroke. They're close. Maybe even the same." He paused. "You're the painter. I'm just a country doctor."

I laughed and elbowed him. "Yeah, right. Just a country doctor. And this is just an old cane pole." I slapped my rod tip out in front of him on the water, splashing him.

We laughed back to the boat, remembering a time when my brother Kevin had his rod tip bitten off by a particularly curious shark and spent the day trying to cast with what was left of his rod. We unstaked the boat in the last of the day, and as he turned it for home, he spoke, almost as if to himself. "You're going to be just fine down here, just fine."

When they left the next morning, I walked around the house. Mom had made sure I was fully unpacked, and the house looked and smelled very clean. Fresh flowers were on the tables. It was quiet, the only sound the distant rush of the sea over the reef. I knew it was time to paint. But the quiet and the blank of the canvas would not let me begin.

I drank coffee and put music on. It was from Dad's Coltrane collection. I turned it up and sat on the veranda in the big chair, looking out at the reef, listening to the night sounds of Alabama.

When I heard Sebastian's skiff arriving at 3 PM, I had not picked up a brush. As he and Veronica walked up the path, I took the blank canvas off the easel and put it face-first against the wall. Veronica gave me a big hug. "How's the artist?"

"Fisherman," Sebastian chimed in, smiling.

"Both. Good."

Veronica brought a pan of crawfish and rice covered in tinfoil.

"This will hold you now. Want me to come in the morning and cook some breakfast?"

"No, I'll just do something simple."

"Okay, but your mom says you're not eating. You look too skinny. You're going to eat down here. We'll send you back healthy."

I laughed and crossed my arms.

Sebastian puttered in the shed, and he spilled some flies out for me on the veranda table to consider for our next day of fishing. Veronica scolded him and told him that I was here to work, not fish. She tried to tidy up some more, but Mom had not left her much to do. By 4:30, I watched them go down on the dock, and their boat buzzed away, leaving it quiet again.

I asked myself if 4:45 was too early for cocktails. I answered myself that it probably was, especially if you hadn't worked at all.

I pulled out the blank canvas. After a moment, I replaced it with another blank canvas. I had brought photos of Downtown Miami, South Beach, the Keys, and Las Olas. Buildings and trees that made me pause to see their lines and reflections. I pinned them on the walls around me.

I thought of Veronica and Sebastian on the dock—his tall figure stooped down to help her up from the boat, her roundness in the bright Androsian dress as she walked up the dock, the late-afternoon light against the cobalt of the sea.

And I began to paint.

I would paint them again many times. On the veranda, on a porch, in the kitchen, on the pier. But that first one remains a personal favorite. Of course, it was not them, only figures like them.

In school, I had been confounded by this. That art was to capture the truth, but only a representation of it. I could not reconcile this and had gone so far as to argue with professors that it was a false idea. They threw the philosophers back at me very hard. I pushed back on what I could see and know. That was what constituted the true and real. If you were capturing the truth, it was untranslated and authentic.

But now, I understood the teachers and philosophers had been right in one important way. When I painted Veronica and Sebastian, it was not them, but a truth of them, in that moment, never to be again, perhaps not even present then. I painted only the truth I saw, and only what my hand and eye could capture.

They would not have expressed it this way, but I think it is why they never asked if it was them. Nor did they ever show a recognition of the scene, or their presence in it. They would just nod and smile and praise it as beautiful.

Except for the water. Sebastian would say, "Very good. That is just the way it comes onto the reef." He knew the water too well to not acknowledge it as true.

I think perhaps that I should have thanked them. Or asked if it was okay. Or said, "It's you!" or "Do you like it?" But I was afraid to touch the thing I had found in case it went away. If they objected or showed shyness or misgiving, I knew it would be gone. So, I said nothing. I just kept painting.

I painted off the cay, too, in Red Bays. Over the years, I had traveled down the straight ribbon of black asphalt to this tiny village. To pick up a worker or guide with Dad. To buy the woven straw baskets or hats with my mom. Where the road ran out, the people lived in a cluster of houses along the edge of the ocean. Escaped slaves and descendants of the Seminole Indians who had crossed the Florida Strait lived isolated and independent until the road was built in the 1930s. The men fished, and the women weaved, and their quiet lives had changed very little.

Over a month of mornings, I painted the traps and fishing skiffs and men loading and unloading on the old concrete pier. I painted the ladies at their weaving. One old beauty, Isabelle, arrested my eye. Her high cheekbones framing gray eyes spoke of her forebears. She agreed to sit for me for an hour each day as I sketched and painted her. At first, it was to be a pose looking squarely into the artist. But she was not natural at rest, and there was no light in her. So, I asked her if she could weave while I sketched and painted. Her eyes were alight as her hands flew over the reeds, her colorful hair wrap framing her bowed head, Roman nose, and high cheeks. When I finished, I knew I had captured that beauty, and it made me very happy.

I woke early each morning. I went right to work in the front room, stopping only for coffee and some toast. By midday, I was spent. I'd sometimes fish in the afternoon. Sebastian would call or stop by to check in. Veronica came every few days, bringing a little food, tidying up. I was most often alone with the sea and the house and the canvases .

I painted the flies Sebastian had spilled on the veranda table. I spent weeks trying to catch the tapered feathers, pop eyes, and sharp hooks. To capture the golds and oranges and subtle browns in the different light passing over the porch through the day. I was not sure I had succeeded—the colors seemed to elude me. I struggled to make a thing that was meant to look alive, not inert. But I tried the flies many times and felt I got closer with each canvas.

CHAPTER 14

MOM AND DAD CAME after a month. Dad was, I know, anxious to fish. But he had left me alone to work. I knew that Mom was anxious to check on me. They had both checked their desire to be there for my good.

When she walked slowly around the front room of the house and saw the work I had done, she only shook her head and smiled. Then she turned to me and hugged me, saying only, "So beautiful." And then looking back at the work, she said, "Oh my."

My mother did not cry, so when I saw tears welling in her eyes, I knew that the paintings were very good.

I took four back to Bernard the next month. He did not cry or hug me, but I could tell he was very pleased. He said they were very good and would definitely sell. And they did. I put what he thought were my best into a juried art exhibition and festival at South Beach.

The painting inspired by beautiful Isabelle weaving in Red Bays won first prize. They even wrote a little piece about me and the painting in the *Herald*. It would sell for $3,000. Originally, I had tried to pay her something for sitting for me, but she had adamantly refused. When I returned, I drove over to Red Bays and told her one of the paintings of her had sold for a lot of money. I pressed three 100-dollar bills into her hand. She tried to decline it, but when I insisted, she tucked them into her dress, simply saying, "Oh, okay," and turned back to her weaving.

All of this was not enough to return me to Brickell. I was back on the cay for another month of work. But the time was broken up. Dad came and fished twice on the weekends. At the end of the month, my brother Kevin came to fish.

He walked around the front room with his rum, gazing into the paint trays and picking up the trowel and brushes. With his dark hair and green eyes, he looked like Mom, but his hands were like Dad's, with long, thin fingers. The brush looked uncomfortable in his hand. He smiled at me. "You do this all day?"

"Not all day. I work in the mornings, then take a break, usually. I sometimes do a little more in the late afternoon when the light is good."

"And fish the rest of the time?"

"No!" I was laughing.

"I don't know how you do it. I would go crazy out here."

I knew this was true. But I did not agree.

We fished with Sebastian the next day. The wind was up, and it was hard to see the fish. We caught nothing in the morning but enjoyed a good lunch and a beer.

Kevin had been a very keen angler in middle school. He begged to go over to the cay with Dad whenever he could, and he haunted the canals and bulkheads around our neighborhood, catching snook and snapper on a fly. He'd get home at dark, sunburned, with filthy feet and a battered fly rod tucked under his arm.

But around his first year in high school, Kevin realized he was handsome and a good basketball player. These two realizations left very little time for fishing. He went from begging to accompany Dad to the cay to sulking when he had to go.

He never fully returned to fishing. Sports and girls were replaced by studies and girls, and then medicine and girls. Then, seemingly just medicine. I knew Dad was proud that he had pursued medicine and done so well, but I wasn't sure he ever forgave him for leaving fishing so far behind.

Kevin remembered this place, Hog Cay flat. He gestured with his sandwich. "I got caught on that edge in deep water. Tide was incoming. Dad had told me not to go across the creek, but it looked plenty shallow to me. Thirty minutes later, the creek was over my shoulders. And a nice six-foot bull shark cruising around."

He laughed a little and took another bite of his sandwich. I couldn't tell what kind of smile was behind his sunglasses.

"Dad wouldn't let Sebastian come get me. Made me fish all the way around the backside of the cay and meet them at the other end." He shook his head.

I remembered. When he and Dad came home from that weekend, Kevin told Mom. She was upset.

"Jack, he's fifteen. You have him out there alone."

"He wasn't alone. We were right there."

"You were half a mile away. He's still a boy."

"He's old enough to know better than to cross deep water on a rising tide. It was a good lesson."

I don't know if it was a good lesson. I only know that Kevin did not return to the cay for nearly a year after that, and then came only with the whole family, fishing very little.

He said none of this as we finished our lunch. He grabbed his rod and turned to Sebastian. "Alright, Sebastian, where are all these fish I keep hearing about?"

They set off on a stalk, and I followed, fishing slowly. The tide had turned to outgoing, and now we saw small sets. Kevin lost two but then found his rhythm, hooking four nice fish in less than an hour. He and Sebastian were laughing and talking, and I could tell he was enjoying himself, and I was glad.

We fished hard that day and the next. On the second evening, he wanted to go out. Going out meant only one thing in our corner of North Andros. A trip over to the only place in Morgan's Bluff, the Waterfront.

We ran the skiff around JoAnna Point in the early evening and tied the bowline to the battered remnants of a short dock. At 7 PM on a Saturday, the Waterfront was hopping, the music loud through the open doors. A group sat on the open-air porch around a game of dominoes.

Through the doors, the single inside room was filled by a pool table and a bar. I had not been out at night since I arrived, but the bartender remembered me from the last time I had been in with Dad. She nodded at me. "What can I get you?" We ordered Kaliks.

The owner, Bobby, came out of the back. "Kit, how you doing? How's your dad?"

He looked at Kevin. "This brother? This the fishing one? Where you been?" They shook hands with the Bahamian grip. It had been long enough that I doubted Bobby knew which brother by name, but he greeted him warmly.

We had barbecued chicken and ribs, and Kevin laughed and flirted with the girls who cooked it, saying he remembered them from when we were all little. We had another round, and Kevin joined the dominoes game.

It was a typically loud affair, tiles clicking, hands slamming, big laughter, and shouts. There was a bottle of rum and a pitcher of water at the table. Kevin was out of practice, and he was beaten easily. They said I needed to take his place. I knew better and instead went out on the other porch to get some fresh air.

The stars were out, and the little harbor was still like glass. I saw the usual weathered fishing boats, some used local skiffs, a fat trawler, and a clean white Yellowfin 31 I had never seen before.

When I went back to the game, three girls were watching. I knew Latrice from when she and her sisters used to swim at the cay. She bumped my hip and put her arm around my shoulder. "Kit! You out with your brother? Where's your dad?" She had been drinking more than beer, and she smiled very big. It was too loud to really talk, and we watched the game for a few minutes.

I finished my beer and decided to have one more while I watched Kevin lose again. I offered to buy one for Latrice and her friends.

I turned to the bar and saw the only other white faces in the place. More accurately, red faces. Three of them. The center one was tall and angular, and he turned as I walked up. His face was red except where his sunglasses had shielded him, leaving a raccoon-like mask. The other two were in fishing shirts, but this one wore a blue-and-white gingham button-down, untucked, and very old boat shoes. Gingham is unusual in North Andros, and exceptionally rare in the Waterfront.

The bar was too small to walk anywhere but that spot, and Gingham, as I called him in my head, smiled at me as I walked up. I nodded, smiled back, and went past them to order. From my brief look at them, I knew several important things. I knew they had come to fish from South Florida. I knew it was their nice new Yellowfin in the harbor. And I knew I was not going to be their tour guide in this little bar in Morgan's Bluff. As I stood at the bar, Gingham just smiled at me, stupidly. Probably drunk. The smallest one spoke first. "So, where are you from?"

Before I could answer, Bobby brought my beers.

"She's from here." Bobby did not smile.

I paid, gave them a nod and my most civil smile, and returned to the game.

One more loss for Kevin, and one more refusal by me to play, and it was time to go. Kevin wanted one more for the road and walked up toward the bar. He spotted the three Americans for the first time. I was heading for the door. Suddenly, big handshakes and greetings broke out. He knew them. Or at least he knew Gingham.

"Kit, you need to come meet these guys!" Kevin didn't drink very much these days. But tonight, not being on call combined with his low tolerance made him a little loud and a bit slurry.

I walked over with what I hoped was a pleasant but unenthusiastic smile.

"These guys are from Vero. This is Patrick, and Todd, and . . ."

The other one put his hand out. "Kyle, nice to meet you." The hand was cold and wet from the beer.

"My sister, Kit."

I nodded. "Catherine, nice to meet you, too."

"Yeah, Patrick is good friends with Dean Willingham. You know Dean, my class? Sister was your year, went to Aquinas?"

I recalled no Willinghams. Gingham was Patrick. He looked at me and smiled in a way that said he was not drunk but knew the others were. He reached out and shook my hand. His hand was not wet and not cold.

"So, you're not from here?" He nodded his head toward the bar and Bobby.

Kevin interrupted, "Yes, she is! Aren't you, Kit? Uh . . . Catherine?"

"Yeah, well, I'm here right now, full-time."

The other two looked dazed and were clearly not following. But Patrick nodded. "What are you doing here?"

"Working."

Kevin chipped in again. "She's painting. She's a painter." He was not so drunk as to miss the puzzled looked on their faces.

"Art painter. Artist."

They nodded. Patrick looked at me directly with gray eyes. "It must be a nice place to paint. I've been doing a little sketching myself."

I was too surprised to respond to a sunburnt fishing guy in the Waterfront talking about sketching. The music was very loud, and I decided I'd misheard him. But I just nodded.

"Couple of very interesting buildings in Nicholls Town. That old stone one on the waterfront?" He *had* said sketching. I knew the building. I nodded. "You know the history of it?"

I did. "Yeah, it was the Symonette house. The first premier of the Bahamas. Big family here. There's a marker in town."

"Very interesting."

The other two had clearly had enough of sketching and prime ministers and were asking Bobby for rum shots and grabbing Patrick's shoulder to turn him to the bar. He looked at me and smiled apologetically.

Kevin wanted to stay.

"One more, Kit?"

I knew a fork in the road at 9:45 PM when I saw one.

"Come on, Kev, back to the cay. Long run in the dark."

I hooked Kevin's arm and nodded at the three boys. As I pulled him away, Kevin reached out and shook their hands.

"Yeah, you guys come out to the cay sometime."

The other two were taking the rums from Bobby, who looked peeved.

Patrick nodded at us both. "I'd love to see it sometime."

Moonlight illuminated Pleasant Harbor as we turned around JoAnna Point. We ran outside the inner reef in a light chop, the night air cold enough for me to be grateful for the fleece I wore. I knew I might be in trouble when I found myself thinking not about the reef but instead about a guy with a red face and a gingham shirt who brought a sketch pad to fish in North Andros.

The weather blew up that night, and it was too blustery to fish. The next morning, we drove down to Fresh Creek for Mass and had breakfast at the hotel. Then I drove Kevin to the airport. It was a lot of time on the empty roads, and we were quiet for much of it. I asked if he would bring his girlfriend Christina to the cay.

"Are you kidding? She'd hate it."

"But she fishes?"

"Yeah, if she has to! She'd go crazy on a rock like that. Nothing to do." He shook his head, and I knew he was right about Christina.

We picked up cell service at the airport. He was checking his phone. He laughed. "Well, that didn't take long!"

"What?" I pulled the old Suburban up to the shed.

"That guy last night, Patrick. He called Willingham from Bimini when they stopped for breakfast this morning. Wanted to know who you are. You don't remember her? Sarah, I think it was?"

"No, Kevin. No recollection of any Sarahs. Or Willinghams."

"He's an architect. Good guy. What should I tell him?"

"Tell who?"

"Willingham. To tell Patrick. About you. What should I tell him?"

He was out of the truck now, grabbing his duffel bag from the back.

"Tell him I'm busy."

He smiled and shook his head.

"And tell him I'm a really good fly fisherman."

He laughed. "Yeah, well, that second part is true!" and he turned toward the tarmac and the waiting plane.

CHAPTER 15

I GOT A CELL PHONE call ten days later. Patrick was going to be in Andros again in a week. Would I mind if he stopped by to see the island?

"Well, you're very welcome. It's not much."

"Well, I've heard it's beautiful. I'd love to see it."

The next Sunday, I saw the white Yellowfin picking its way through the gap in the inner reef. Inside the reef was deep, but the passage was just over two feet at low tide. It was high enough now that he was able to make his way through. It took him fifteen minutes to cover the half mile with the boy on the bow sighting for depth and coral heads. Once they were inside the reef, I didn't watch.

When they were at the dock, I went down to take the bowline.

He wore a white oxford shirt, untucked, and faded madras shorts. He looked pretty dressed up for fishing. He had his sketch pad. He introduced his friend, Will. He looked up at the house.

"It's beautiful."

"Very simple."

"Who designed it?"

"My dad. I mean, he had some help from a friend at home, but he did the sketches himself and planned it all."

He raised his eyebrows and nodded. "Impressive."

As we walked up to the house, he turned to me and said, "I brought a different friend." He smiled, and I laughed.

He sketched the house, getting very sweaty in his oxford shirt. They were staying up at Chub Cay, thirteen miles north. They'd fished hard for two days in the pocket and were heading home the next morning. He said the fishing had been fair, raising a marlin and some sails. They brought some dolphin for me in a Ziploc bag.

We walked around the cay. Will grabbed a cast net and hunted for pogeys in a rocky pool on the edge of the island. Patrick told me about his architectural practice. He worked for a firm in Miami, doing a mix of commercial and residential. He did not sound enthused. He tapped his sketch pad and looked up at the house. "I like this kind of work. Really good things, thoughtful, classic. Really well done, but you gotta make a living."

I told him I knew all about it and described my time at the agency. He wanted to start his own firm, maybe in Palm Beach, doing classical work throughout Florida. I thanked him for the fresh fish.

"It's a treat. We don't do a lot of blue water."

"So, you fly-fish?"

I nodded.

"Beautiful flats around here."

"Yeah, it's pretty amazing."

"So I hear. We tried the flat up at Chub. Saw some fish. Not much luck."

"Well, the guide matters."

"Yeah. I'm sure. They said the Joulters are the ticket."

I looked around at the reef and the flats beyond. "Yeah. A lot of fish." I looked back at him and said, "Do you fly-fish much?"

"Yeah. Well, I'm learning. It's hard." He smiled and laughed at himself. I liked him more just for that.

We had a beer on the veranda. Will went back down to putter in the boat.

"Pretty far out of the way. It was very nice of you guys to come down and visit."

"Well, I'm willing to make a trip for great architecture. This is really pretty. Really unique."

"How often do you get to Andros?"

"Not very often."

He smiled at the floor and his beer.

"This is only my second time on Andros, actually."

And he looked up and smiled at me, and we both laughed.

The tide was going out, and they had to go. He shook my hand at the dock. Not even a hug. Maybe I hadn't made the impression I'd hoped to.

But he called the next week. There were more calls, and I had a reason to be in South Florida the following week. We both liked the same Cuban joint in the Art's District. We talked until 1 AM. I went back more often. It seemed different and more alive, and I wasn't sure if it was my time on the cay, or him. I decided it was probably both. He came to one of my exhibits. He picked quirky art movies that I liked. We sketched together.

He met my parents and didn't run. My brothers were glad to see someone who actually fished, and Kevin already liked him. We fly-fished together on Biscayne Bay, and he was not half bad. He was learning, and he wanted to learn more. After a few months, I thought Mom liked him so much that she deliberately decided to say nothing.

He went to my exhibit. He could be serious with his glass of wine and intelligent criticism. But he would roll his eyes afterward with me, talking about the gathering of art characters and their pompous comments on the paintings. I sold everything from that exhibit at full price, and we decided that characters with money to spend on art were worth hanging around with.

He usually called me Catherine, but when it was just the two of us, sometimes, he called me Kit. I liked that he knew when to use each.

He urged me to do a self-portrait. I'd never even considered it. He cited artists that had. He'd done his homework. I demurred. He said it was part of being a real artist.

"What, with a mirror? That's creepy."

He laughed. "No, in your mind's eye. What does that look like?"

I decided it looked like a girl on a porch, with a fly rod propped in the corner, a glass of wine in hand, stretched out on a rattan lounge at the end of the day, her body in repose, tired, and comfortable, showing the satisfaction of having worked well and fished well.

When I finished it, I knew it was that moment. I could feel and see it in the paint and the lines. And it was like me, but it was not me. It was just how I thought it would look if someone came out of the house to find me on that day. So, I did not call it a self-portrait. I just called it *Girl on the porch*.

I liked it very much. I tried to keep it—this one for only me—but Bernard insisted that keeping work for myself could stunt my artistic growth. Plus, he loved it and wanted to sell it. Maybe, down the road, he said, I could gather a few favorites for myself, but not now. There was too much left to do. I would sell it.

Before it went on display in the gallery, Patrick bought it. It was there in his living room when I came over for dinner. He had persuaded Bernard to let him have it. It took some coaxing.

"At first, he said it wasn't for sale. I don't even think he remembered me. He said he didn't know you had a boyfriend."

"I don't talk to Bernard about my love life."

"I had to pay full price."

"Good. I'm a starving artist."

"You're skinny, but you're not starving."

"Why buy this one?"

He looked at it for a long moment, then slowly counted his reasons on his fingers. "It's perfect. It makes me happy just to look at it. And I think I can appreciate it." Then he turned, looked directly into my eyes, and said, "Maybe more than anyone."

I knew that was true.

2015

CHAPTER 16

HE HAD BEEN ASKING when I would be down to fish. He said I needed to bring the children. I laughed and told Dad to tell him I'd be down for the next good tide. But I waited one tide too long.

I was old enough to know that phone calls in the middle of the night are almost never good. And this one was bad.

Sebastian was gone. Heart attack. Dad's voice sounded flat. I was drowsy. I made him repeat it. Then my mom was on the line. Talking about Veronica. Recounting her call and Veronica crying. When Mom's voice caught, I teared up too. Veronica's grief reached across the Gulf Stream all the way to Vero Beach.

Patrick sat up and turned the bedside light on. He could hear enough to know. He got up to make coffee. Dad was telling me he had a flight the next day. He had to get across to see Veronica. The funeral would be Friday.

I had not seen him in six months. I had not fished with him, or even been to the cay, more than three times in two years. So, I had missed him. And now that part of things was gone.

I sat in my robe through dawn on the back porch—thinking about what I'd been doing that made me too busy to go see Sebastian. Or Veronica. Or the cay. Too busy to tilt my face up to the sun and see the vast flats and endless sky.

It was easy to say *children*. That's what all our friends would've said, and simply stopped at that. Three children. It was enough to say that this meant *too busy* to have any life apart from them. Far too busy to fish, and certainly too busy to go away for a fishing weekend.

Eight, six, and four. These were needy ages. Boy, girl, girl. There was swim practice, school projects, lacrosse. Carpooling to orchestrate for them all.

But the truth was that I had inherited from both my parents a discipline and fierce energy that meant I could manage my days and run our lives and keep my children and house in some order. Patrick had built us a house smack-dab in the middle of Old Vero where he grew up.

Our life was all around us, close and easy. My car rarely recorded 100 miles in a month. I had a mother-in-law I liked who helped. Mom was there often, on a weekend or a day trip.

But no matter the available and trusted hands, and the well-checked lists, I could not imagine going away. Not even a day or two. To fish or sit. The very suggestion sounded ridiculous.

I could not even find time to paint. I had a studio. It was a space of big windows and white light that opened to the water behind the house. I had enjoyed making it, with sketches and clipped pictures. With Patrick. It was just for me. Not as *wife* or *mom*. As *artist*. He wanted that for me.

But building it did not make it so. The beautiful space yielded no art. I sat before blank canvases and did not paint. I drank coffee. I made lists. I enjoyed the quiet break from the children (not allowed in by strict order of their father). I felt guilty. About being in there. About producing nothing. After a few months of false starts, I avoided the space.

I lost myself in the children and the house. A year passed. I had painted nothing. I told myself the children were my art. Sometimes, I believed it.

My last time fishing with Sebastian had been the year before. It was Dad's birthday, and Charlie and Kevin and my mom and I all came down for a weekend. Our spouses had the child duty, but I knew only Patrick regretted not being there.

There was cell service on the cay now. To me, it meant I could check on things. Patrick's mother was with him to help. He still sounded overwhelmed. I gave advice on what the youngest one wanted. I was talking about cutting the crust off grilled cheese.

We were out on the veranda. Dad was ignoring all of this. He was at the table with some line, a reel, and small pliers. But Mom was listening. "They're fine. Let's go fish."

Mom wanted to help. She did not push to fish. I did not need to be pushed to fish. I collected myself.

"Sure, I'm ready," I said as brightly as I could, putting the grilled cheese out of my mind.

Sebastian looked around at us on the veranda—his brown eyes now beneath more salt than pepper and his old, blue fishing hat. He looked at my brother, who was fiddling with his newly bought Orvis flats pack.

"Charlie, you fishing much?"

"A little bit. Not enough. Work gets in the way."

"Can't do that. You need to come see us more. Come spend a week."

I knew this was impossible. Charlie was running a busy surgery practice and raising two middle school kids. His wife, Melissa, did not fish. But Charlie inherited good manners.

"I need to, I know. Got to get my life better organized."

Dad came out of the house to hear this, and added, "That's right. More fishing. It'll make you a better surgeon, better dad, better husband. Right, Margaret?"

My mom gave a chuckle that did not sound amused. "I'm sure it's good for surgery."

Dad ignored it, just looking around at us. He said, "Ready to go?"

We had the whole afternoon, and the summer days were long, so we ran far north to a flat called Bird that dad loved. Two low, broken lines of sand and scrub reached out to the ocean, framing a wide, white, shallow flat. The fish came off the edges on the change of tide. You could wait and cast as they picked their way toward you.

It would be easy for Mom. She was a good and strong wader. She could cast. But there was a lack of force in her casting hand that made a flutter. This place would suit her with short casts and lots of shots.

Mom and Dad rode with Sebastian. My brothers and I were in the other skiff that he borrowed from his nephew. I could not recall the last time all of us had fished together. Maybe high school for me, and college for the boys. We staked the boats together at the end of the flat. Dad and Sebastian conferred off to the side for a moment, nodding toward the edges of the flat, then at each other in agreement. I watched them, observing what would happen while everyone else messed with their gear in the boats.

Sebastian turned to the four of us and said, "Miss Margaret, you and Kit come with me. You boys fish with your dad."

It sounded like "Dodd" in his Andros accent.

Charlie and Kevin needed a guide. I did not need a guide and had not for a very long time. I was still on the girl team.

I would catch more fish, and they'd credit Sebastian. I thought fondly of the cell phone in my bag but recalled that there was no service on this distant flat. Patrick and his mom were with the kids.

I took a breath. The phone was a dead brick. The flat was alive and present. I nodded to my mom, and we walked up into it.

I think Sebastian was seventy-four that year. His long frame had always moved slowly, now slower. But he had the same posture—leaning forward, one arm tucked behind him, dark eyes beneath the ragged blue cap sweeping the flat for signs of fish.

The boys worked the left edge together, where the water deepened in a long, narrow blue crease. I saw them casting to fish there, with no signs of catching. They grew distant as we moved further right.

Mom was walking close to me and talking, which Sebastian did not like. He wanted us to watch the water and see for ourselves. But he would not growl at my mother like he would at me. He just walked further ahead of us.

We stalked the edge on the right, and it was empty. But after a few dozen yards, we saw water pushing and some splashes up ahead. Sebastian pointed at the fish. I saw and stopped still. When Mom kept talking, he raised his hand like a stop signal. She saw it and stopped midsentence. I glanced over at her, and she had a small smile. She saw the fish. They made me smile too.

Sebastian motioned us forward, me to the left, Mom to the right. He did not need to tell me that Mom would take a shot first. He and I knew I would not need many chances and could freely give this first one of the day to her.

But, like I had worried, Mom's cast was made after one too many false casts. It fluttered harmlessly fifteen feet from the fish.

"Too short." Sebastian's hoarse whisper told the obvious.

"Take it in now. Try again." She pulled the line, too fast.

"Slowly now." She cast again, closer that time.

"Strip, strip . . ."

The fish moved away, not noticing the fly.

"Got to get it closer now. Try again."

She did. The fish passed near, but not close enough. They moved past us and were gone.

"Shoot. Sorry. Thought I had them on that last one." It was the closest she could come to cussing. So I knew she was disappointed. Mostly for us. We said it was okay and moved further up the edge.

I looked across the flat to see Kevin work a fish, his casting rhythm and smooth stroke apparent even from this distance. There was a splash, followed by the movement of a catch. Before he brought the fish close to release it, I looked up the flat and moved ahead toward the next sign of fish.

Mom was walking close now again. She was talking about her friend Barbara's tennis injury and her suspicion that she might have the same issue with her own knee. I glanced over at her.

Still beautiful under a ball cap and sunglasses, slim in her khakis and fishing shirt, just now really showing age at sixty-four. I recalled the girl in the mirror that morning with the big bags under her eyes and the tight feel of my fishing pants and decided she just might look better than me.

Sebastian was now far ahead. He stopped still, which meant fish. I saw them, four moving slowly off the edge and onto the flat, feeding greedily into the shallow. It would be easy to put it in front of them. Sebastian motioned us forward.

"You go, Kit."

"No, Mom, you go."

"I've gone. Catch one."

I would not say no twice. I moved up next to Sebastian. He smiled with his lips pursed, half happy I came up, half calling me out on what we both knew was my greed to fish, pushing in front of Mom.

He pointed. "Just left on that first one now."

I already had my rod moving, line back, singing in the air. I saw the spot, and the fly was there. It was a solid cast, considering it was my first time in nine months.

The second fish moved toward it suddenly, then tipped up, all tail and fin. I strip set, and he was on, exploding in a swirl of silver and blue. The others fled in three directions.

He was a big fish, and I let him run off the flat into the deeper edge. Sebastian gave a low growl of approval, correcting nothing, saying, "Whoa, whoa, yes, he's a good one."

Mom was up with me now, laughing.

"That's it, Kit."

He ran twice, and then he was in, and Sebastian had him. He looked up at me, smiling.

"We need a picture of this. Your children need to see this one."

I held my catch just out of the water, up next to Sebastian. Mom took the photo with her phone.

"We're sending it to Patrick. John will love it."

My oldest was a fisherman. But he had not bonefished with me. I'm not sure he believed all the stories Patrick and my dad told him about my fishing. I was a force of carpool and laundry, not fly-fishing. This would help.

We revived the big fish and released him, and he glided away in a silver swirl. Sebastian turned to me. "Yes. You need to get him down to fish with us."

I laughed. "He's eight. He may not be ready for this."

"Sure. He ready. He ready. Just get him here so he can learn. You started at ten!"

"Yeah, and look how I turned out."

"He could be better than his mom!"

Then he turned, laughing, up into the flat.

Mom missed several more, and then she caught one at the very end of the flat. I caught three more. Surprisingly, the wind was still flat enough to fish. I saw a few more pairs, but they refused a poorly placed fly. I was rusty.

Sebastian let me off. "Light and water changed. They not eating."

It was not the casting or stripping.

"Good. Thought I lost my touch."

"No, you fished very well. You just need to be down here more!"

Mom answered for me, laughing, "She's busy raising babies, Sebastian!"

He just kept walking a few steps ahead of us, arm tucked behind him. He shook his big head. "I know. Time goes. It goes."

We met the boys at the boats. They were laughing about a terrible miss Charlie had.

"The fish practically ran into you, Charlie." Dad was laughing with a beer in his hand, his face smeared with zinc, a buff around his neck.

"He was too close to cast!" Charlie said in his defense.

I looked at the three of them. "How'd you guys do?"

"I told you that's the first thing she'd say." Kevin was lying back on the forward deck of the skiff, his hat pulled partly over his eyes, smiling to the sky.

"What? How'd you do?"

Charlie now chimed in, "But who's counting, right?"

"We always count."

"Not since we were like twelve."

Dad shook his head and laughed. "We're not afraid. Kevin caught two, Charlie caught none, and Dad caught one. You?"

"Well, just saying, the two Mom's caught five between us. So, that's something."

Charlie added, as I expected, "And Sebastian. Don't forget Sebastian."

But Sebastian would not have it. "No, your sister's like the guide now. And your mom had a nice fish."

The boys could tease no more with Sebastian's pronouncement.

I stood beside Dad on the run home. After all these years, he knew the channels well enough to lead, but he let Sebastian go first. The light was falling to our right, in a broad canvas of pink and gray. We had rum in metal Yeti cups, and it felt warm to my center in the chill of the wind.

We only talked a little over the wind and the engine—about his work and my house and kids. The short sentences were enough between the two of us now, after all these years.

Then he said the word "retire" and I wanted him to stop the boat. We needed full paragraphs for that word. We did not stop, and he just looked forward, speaking over the noise. "Just thinking about it. When it's time." Then a long pause. Something I couldn't hear, then he continued, "Might retire." I could not see his eyes through the sunglasses to see how sincere this was. He did not look old enough to be retired.

We were there to celebrate his sixty-fifth birthday. My friends' parents were calling sixty the new fifty. He was the head of one of the largest surgery groups in Fort Lauderdale. He did not golf. Retirement was not a word I had ever heard from him. Nor was it one I expected.

At dinner, we did not speak of retirement—only fishing and medicine and politics. We sat in the candlelight and talked about who looked like who. It was a favorite childhood game. It was usually settled that Kevin looked like Mom, and her beauty did make for a handsome dark-haired boy. I looked like Dad, and his Irish nose and sandy hair made for a cute and sporty tomboy sort of girl. As for Charlie, we wavered over the years but usually decided he was an amalgam of the two—my father's nose with my mom's green eyes and high cheekbones. Or perhaps he was a copy of my mom's father. It depended on the light and, now that we were older, how much wine we had.

We toasted the absent spouses—Charlie's Madeline, who would never fish, Kevin's Melissa, who would fish if she had to, and my Patrick, who had earned his way into our circle through practice, focus and, according to my brothers, some discrete but critical brownnosing of Dad and Sebastian.

I had addressed this last accusation forcefully in Mom and Dad's kitchen several years earlier, explaining the difference between respectful engagement and being a sycophant. They agreed to stop openly mentioning it, but not to withdraw the accusation.

The next morning after breakfast, Mom and Dad put us in the skiff and ran us to the dock. They would stay on through Tuesday. Sebastian was there, and we piled into his old truck and headed south to the airport.

It was quiet as pine stands and scattered houses flashed past. Sebastian spoke when we pulled up to the old metal roofs of the airport. "You all need to come back now. Need to fish more." We all said we would.

When he handed me my duffel, he looked squarely at me and said, "You need to come back. And bring that boy now. *Time.*"

Just that single word, and he was back in the truck and pulling away, heading north to the sea.

CHAPTER 17

I HAD NEVER WORN a dress on Andros. But I had one on that day. I drew the line at pantyhose, and Mom fussed at me for it. I might have been the only woman in church without them.

An Andros funeral is a formal affair. People you are accustomed to seeing around the island in their work and fishing clothes, or maybe shorts and shirts in the evening, are dressed in their best suits and ties (and sometimes tie pins and pocket squares) for boys and men. Formal dresses and hose (and sometimes hats) for girls and women.

We heard the music first, a tuba, a trombone, and two trumpets. It was a jazzy swing sound, with just a trace of island melancholy. The musicians walked up the bright, hot road, and Veronica and her two sons followed. Behind them was the long black Cadillac hearse.

In a place of large funerals, this one was far too big for the old Methodist church in Nicholls Town. It was gray stone with edges dressed in conch-shell tabby. Sebastian's cousin Ruben was the pastor, and Veronica's grandfather had helped build it.

The sun was high and bright, and it was already very hot at 10 AM. People crowded under tents on the lawn and on the street outside. Women in bright-green, pink, and canary-yellow dresses splashed around the lawn and porch, cooling themselves with straw fans, and they still shined dark and lovely. Men huddled in suits of gray and blue, with patches of bright color, talking.

We were on the edge of the crowd, and Dad went to get something in the truck. Then Freddy was there. He was his mom's son that day, round and bright, greeting us with a smile in the face of mourning. He hugged us all. I could see the signs that he had been crying, but he was not now.

"Mom asked me to come get you. You're going in with us."

Dad came forward. "Hey, Freddy." They had a big hug and shook hands.

"Tell your mom we're fine out here. You save those spots for family."

"No, she said, Doc. After you finish on the casket, you sit with us. You have to do what she says." He flashed a brave smile at Dad.

"Always." Dad smiled a little too.

Freddy led us through the crowd. Dad stopped and shook hands with groups of men and talked briefly, falling behind. We went into the church, into a small room off the entry hall.

Veronica was there, dressed in black, with a hat and veil. She was surrounded by two of her sisters and some cousins I recognized but could not name. Malcolm was talking to the pastor. He was very tall and getting a little gray like his dad.

She lifted up her veil and gave us all a big Veronica smile, but with tears. Mom hugged her first, I was next, and she worked her way through my brothers behind me. She held Dad out at arm's length, and just shook her head, still smiling, her throat catching. They didn't say anything then, and I knew Dad was trying not to cry.

Luckily for him, Malcolm was there now, greeting us all. He had a deep voice, and he was shaking hands and talking almost like a song. "Oh, the O'Neills! Morning. Hard morning."

We all nodded.

The wake had been very quick, the night of his death, so we had not been able to make it down. They took us into the next room to see him in the casket. His color was gone, and he looked crammed into the suit and narrow casket. But he looked very peaceful. We followed Dad's example and took turns kneeling on the little wood step. When my turn came, I could not think of anything to pray for. He was very gone, but I knew he was all right. So I just tried to say hello.

Freddy walked us to the second row of pews. They had saved a little space for us to sit between the cousins and siblings. The church was packed and hot, and the people talked quietly. There was a little humming from the choir up front, warming up, and little snuffling cries from behind us.

Then the music started. It was a piano and horns, and it had the sound of a march in a blues club. The casket was wheeled up, and I saw Dad's sunburnt face amongst the Conch Sound men walking with it. He stared straight ahead into a distant place, and I knew he was trying to be clear eyed and steady handed.

The pastor read from St. Luke's account of the apostles catching far too many fish for their nets, and from St. John's telling of Jesus calming the sea and storm. He talked about each of them, and how it was no accident that Christ chose fishermen—men who knew the sea, who had the faith to set out into it, and to call upon a God who would hold them in His palm, that He willed it, providing a catch and a safe harbor at day's end. I smiled a little to myself because I knew that was just how Sebastian would have described it. I had heard him say that very thing.

Then he read from St. John's gospel, when the apostles went to fish and returned to find Jesus on the beach, grilling fish for breakfast.

"And so it is for our brother, Sebastian. He has returned to the beach, and he sits down with the Lord to laugh and talk, sharing stories of his day, and sharing a meal. And his catch. And his life. Welcomed home on the distant shore."

I was sitting next to Dad, and he was smiling a little and wiping tears away. I was not able to hold it together any longer. He took my hand, and Mom reached across him and squeezed both our hands.

Then the choir sang the hymn "Oh God Our Help in Ages Past" with a rhythm and gusto I had never heard. The congregation swayed with the music. Even my dad and my brothers swayed, and they were not swaying kind of people.

Malcolm gave a eulogy. He was the principal of the high school in Fresh Creek. He was comfortable talking and could be trusted by his mother not to cry. He looked around at the packed church and flattened his notes on the rostrum. "My dad would have loved to see you all."

A man called from the back of the church, "He does see us!" And the crowd laughed.

"Yes, he does, yes, he does." Malcolm smiled and nodded. "Because he loved this place. He loved its people. All of you. He loved his family. And he loved the sea. He lived his life and those things. He lived every day for those things. And for all of us. For his family. For his friends." He gestured around to the crowd. There were many amens from the crowd to his remarks.

"And he loved the Lord. As Pastor told you, he knew his Lord and prayed every day." There were more amens from the crowd.

"He prayed at home. And out on the flats. He saw the Lord's hand in everything. The good, and the bad. The happy, and the sad. The catching, and the breaking down!" At this, the crowd laughed again.

"He made a very loving home for my mom and my brothers and me. He was a good provider. And a good father. They loved us enough to take the strap to us if we were bad!" The crowd laughed at this too. "But luckily, that wasn't too often. He's the reason Freddy and I have done okay." He nodded at his brother in the front row, who nodded back.

"More than anything, he loved my mom." Even steady Malcolm had to pause to collect himself before going on at this point. "That was clear to us when we were little, and right up through this very day." He just nodded, and paused again, perhaps deciding not to say more at the risk of breaking down.

"Mom and Freddy and I are very grateful to all of you. The whole Stewart family thanks you. Your prayers, and your kindnesses. Your food, your hugs, and your tears have made this bearable."

He paused, eyeing the crowd before continuing, "People have come from all over the Bahamas and Andros today. And even from further away, from Florida." He looked at us.

"Thank you to Dr. O'Neill and his family for being here today. He loved you and your family, Doc. And you two may have caught more bonefish than any two Andros men ever!" The crowd laughed at this, and I heard a couple of amens.

I was embarrassed for us to be singled out. But my dad just looked calmly at Malcolm and nodded. He was not embarrassed. He was just where he belonged, burying his friend.

The reception afterward was at the old hotel in Conch Sound. There were tents there, too, as shelter against the midday sun. Tables of food and drinks were arrayed. People ate Styrofoam bowls of conch—cracked, salad, and chowder—and talked in small groups.

There was no alcohol, and my brothers and I regretted it. We could have used what my father called the Irish antidote, and we knew he needed one. Instead, we drank Sprite in small glass bottles and talked with old familiar faces around the crowd.

Veronica was surrounded by so many who wanted to pay their respects; I didn't have a moment to get close to her. My brothers managed to catch her, but every time she freed up for a moment, I was across the tent, tied up with someone else.

I had already seen her and would see her soon. I was hot and tired and sad, and needed a drink and some AC. We quietly made our way toward the street and the truck. But as we passed, she caught my eye, in the middle of a crowd, and called to me, "Kit!" She had not called me that child's name in a very long time, preferring Catherine. I went over. She was still smiling, her eyes brimming. She hugged me, and I was ten again, and it was better.

"He said . . . he said . . . you understood it so well! You were like another guide in the boat! You could see it all! You keep that with you now!"

Now I was crying ridiculously, mascara surely running. I put my hand to my eyes and mouth to catch the grief, but I could not. This was not what she needed today, me stupidly crying when she had lost her husband.

But in comforting, she was comforted. "You must come see us now! Bring those children! And that Patrick!" She liked Patrick, and hearing her say it made me glad. I told her I would be down soon.

And I told her I loved her.

And she said she knew.

CHAPTER 18

IT TOOK ME nearly two months, but I kept my promise and came back to see Veronica. It was perhaps the only time I came to the cay in good weather and did not fish. I only had a day with her. She was too busy and disciplined to sit for long, so to talk to her, I had to work. We shook out rugs, mopped, and cleared out two closets full of old clothes and fishing gear. We sorted through what to keep. She'd take the rest to families in town.

I did not know how to cook her curried chicken, though I loved it and had been around her making it for years. So she showed me, and we did it together.

Dad had been over the week before. She said he'd hardly eaten and hardly fished. She was worried about him. It was her essence to be worried about Dad in a time of her own loss. She thought he needed to fish more.

Then she wiped her hands on a dishtowel and turned to me, saying, "What about you? How are you?"

I was okay, and I told her so. She nodded and accepted it. She knew it was not a lie. Then she was quiet and looked at me. "I'm not okay. I'm trying. But it's very hard."

She gave a small and sad smile. It was the first she admitted how hard it was. And it was the only glimpse I would get. She asked for the peppers I chopped and added them to the curry. I did not know what to say, so I told her I was praying for her, and I had been.

"That helps. Thank you. Now let me show you how to turn this."

She grabbed a wooden spatula and guided me closer. She turned the chicken and peppers in the skillet, then let me try it. We didn't talk about her loss anymore that day.

When we walked down to the dock to run her back in the skiff, I told her I was very tired. She laughed and smiled at me. "It's hard work running a house!"

I nodded.

"What about your drawing?" She had always called it that.

"It's fine. Not much time for that."

I had always been a bad liar, and she knew it.

The boat was packed. She turned back to me. "You know what I told you Sebastian said?"

I nodded.

"You can see. He wasn't just talking about fishing."

I was unsure what she meant. She went on.

"The drawing. The fishing. You're here to see. Like your dad. That's a gift. A gift you have."

"Thank you."

She grabbed my hand firmly, then continued, "No. You have that gift. You have to use it. You take care of your family. I know you do that. But it's okay to have something. Something good. That makes you happy. That's for you. Your drawing is that, I think."

"What about you? Your family is everything."

"Well, yes. That's my gift. I've given it freely."

It was true.

"And you have that. But you have this other. Like your dad. He's a good doctor, I know. That's a gift. But he's also a fisherman. And a dad. And a writer."

She paused and looked at the boat, then back at me. "He could have stopped at doctor. Or dad." She smiled now, the warm one that made me glow. "That's you, too, Catherine. Ever since you were little. You have more. So, you use all of that."

"Veronica, I can't even keep up with the laundry!"

We both laughed.

"Laundry will get done. It all gets done. Enjoy your babies and your husband. It all gets done."

She hugged me and got into the boat. I took her across and watched her drive off from the dock in the old pickup truck.

I turned for the cay in the last of the light, thinking about what I was good at, and what to do with it.

CHAPTER 19

THE *RETIREMENT* WORD came up again that year, just a few months after losing Sebastian. Dad brought it up after a Sunday lunch at our house. The kids were swimming, and my parents and I were sitting near the pool deck.

"Big news. I've decided to retire. It's time."

He said it like he was telling himself, like we weren't there. He was picking at his slice of key lime pie.

I wanted to say something sharp, but I tried to wait. I learned I was better when I did that. But it was quiet, and I had to say something.

"Why? I mean, you're young, Dad."

He smiled, closed lipped.

"Ah, not so much, really. Not for a surgeon."

He looked at the pie. I looked to Mom. Retirement would be a happy thing for her. But she looked at him and was not smiling or helping.

"It's time." He said it again, then looked at me and smiled. It was a kind of smile he used when he told a story with a disappointing outcome, like a mistake or a lost fish.

I did not stop.

"How about just slowing down? Maybe fewer cases?"

He shook his head. "No, doesn't work that way. It's time, Kit."

Then he was up, gathering the pie plates and heading for the kitchen. He paused to cheer for my daughter at the end of the diving board, and then went in the house.

I looked at Mom. She raised her eyebrows and gave me a bemused shrug.

"He's going to drive you crazy."

She smiled. "I know. But no. He's got the cay. And we can travel. Somewhere other than a bonefish flat."

"I just don't see why now. I mean, he seems to still be enjoying it."

"Well, it's complicated. It's his call, honey."

It was his call, and he was not going to discuss it with anyone, not even me. When I talked to him on the phone the next week, he just repeated, "It's time." And gave me nothing more.

I should have been happy for him. And for Mom. He had worked very hard and did not need to work anymore. But I had trouble seeing him without his 5 AM drive to the hospital. Without his rounds in the afternoon. Without his cases to talk about over a drink before dinner. I kept thinking of an imbalance and the spinning of a wheel.

I knew I wasn't the only one. I had lunch with Charlie and told him I was having a hard time with this.

"Well, it's not you retiring, Kit." He took a bite of his shrimp and smiled at me.

"I know. But I'm worried about him. You're not worried?"

"Well, he'll have to figure it out. The next chapter. People do that all the time. Even surgeons."

"How many? How successfully? Or happily, maybe?"

"Some. Some successfully. But it's a journey. It's a big change, for sure."

"I just don't get why. Why now? It doesn't make sense."

He didn't respond. He put his fork down.

"I'm not sure I should tell you this, but I think you need to know. I'm not even sure Mom knows."

I could not think of a good thing about Dad that Mom did not know.

"What?"

"He can't practice anymore."

"What? What are you talking about?"

I was going off my chair, over the table, off a ledge.

"He can't, okay?" He was flushed and looked very tight. "I shouldn't tell you. He doesn't want anyone to know. It's embarrassing to him, okay?"

"What are you talking about?"

"He made a mistake. A couple mistakes."

I was still not getting it, not understanding their world and what *mistake* meant. If I made a mistake, I threw the pan away and started over. I could even paint over a mistake on a canvas.

"What mistake? Like he's in trouble?"

"No, no. A mistake with a patient. In surgery. He got something wrong."

"Well, that happens, right? I mean, it's complex; it involves snap judgments."

I had heard them talk about judgment in the moment, heard them ridicule those who second-guessed a surgeon's decision.

"Not Dad. Not like this. It was a very basic thing. He just got it mixed up and did the opposite."

"What happened?"

"It was okay. The nurse stopped it. She said something. Dad agreed, of course. The patient was fine, and it was okay. And the nurse didn't tell anyone. She loves Dad, you know; everyone does down there. He's so respected. So, it's fine. But Dad knew." He paused and looked back up at me. "He was pretty shaken up. I don't think he could tell anyone else. He told me and Kevin. He asked us not to tell anyone."

"Well, this happens, right? I mean, doctors make mistakes?"

"Not like this. Very basic stuff, Kit. It'd be like you painting blue when you knew red was what was needed."

"Well, that's okay. It's a decision."

"No, not a decision. It was wrong. Like using the wrong end of the brush. Maybe not. But close. Dad doesn't do that. Never. So, he's a little afraid."

"But in a whole career? One thing?"

"I think there have been others. He didn't say, but I think there have been others. He caught them himself. Or nothing happened. I mean, no one's been hurt. But he's just a little freaked out. He's a little afraid, I think."

He looked down at his plate now. I felt sick. He looked back up at me. "You know, he's the best. He's my hero. Seriously. My model. You may not know that. But I've watched, I've seen it. He is the very finest surgeon I've ever worked with. In Baltimore, New York, here, anywhere. So, this is very, very difficult. Perfection only has one way to go."

I had heard my dad say this. Seek and achieve perfection. But it only has one way to go. Eventually, it will become imperfect. I responded with another Dad phrase, "Clear eyes and a steady hand." I smiled.

"Yeah. He still has that."

We were quiet. He turned back to his shrimp. Then he looked up and stopped. "I shouldn't have told you. He made us promise not to tell anyone. He's mortified."

"I won't say anything."

"I know. But you shouldn't know. It's not important."

But it was important. And he should not have told me.

I called Mom the next day and tried to casually bring up Dad's retirement. I wanted to see if she would give me some hint that she knew. I wanted to know that he told her this most important thing.

But in my dad's case, you could not bring up retirement casually. She gave me nothing. It was not up for discussion.

"It's time. It's his decision."

These had become the only points.

I saw him a week later. He brought John back from a lacrosse camp and sat for a few minutes in the family room. We had enough small talk that I felt comfortable raising the retirement topic.

"So, you're really doing this retire thing?"

"Yep. It's done. My last day is the end of the month."

I had not known it was done. There was no going back. My mission had no purpose. Unless I wanted to know the reason. But I already knew. And he would never tell me.

"So, what will you do?"

He smiled. "Fish. Write a little. Fish some more. Mom has some big trips planned. You should see the dining room table. Looks like a travel agency showroom."

He was still smiling, and I thought it was a true smile. So I took a chance.

"Won't you miss it? Surgery? Medicine?"

He paused, and the smile lessened.

"Oh yeah. But there is a time to take up the tool and a time to put it down. It's been good. Very good. But it's time for other things."

He changed the subject to my painting, and I knew I would get no more from him.

I had something to tell him about painting. I had two canvases started. I told him I did not think they were very good, but he insisted on taking a look. He said they were a good start.

He praised the light in my studio again. "Such good light. Patrick got that so right. It just feels like art in here."

It was true. The room was lovely and felt full again. Of light. Of good lines. Of peace. I liked to be there. Even if I only painted a little, it did not discourage me.

I'd go in after dropping the kids at school. I'd drink my coffee. Walk around. Mix some paints. It was nice to have two canvases in the works. One always called me. I was never stymied.

I wasn't sure if what I was doing was good, but it felt good to paint again. Each day, a little more. I liked what I saw, but it was too early to tell if they were any good. I told him that.

He looked at them for another long moment, took a big breath, and spoke. "Yeah. It's that way, I think. It's assembling day upon day, moment upon moment, right? We are all like a canvas of many, many strokes. You're just doing that. But literally, right? You work on and don't know whether it's really good until its finished?"

He looked to me for an answer, and I just nodded and smiled, and knew we were not talking about me, or about painting.

CHAPTER 20

MOM HAD ACQUIRED an iPhone that year, and she embraced it. She called me more, often about nothing in particular. I'd be folding laundry or cleaning up breakfast or working on a school project, and she'd call. She discovered that her call showed her name. So if I didn't pick up, she'd call again, assuming I hadn't seen it. I decided that it was generally easier to just pick up.

My dad and his contented retirement had become her project. She made sure he was busy. But he refused to get serious about tennis. He liked to compete, and he was bored with doubles. As someone who had been a very good athlete in his youth, he was irritated at his lack of speed.

At her invitation, grandchildren were frequent visitors at the house. He liked to see them swim, and he'd make pancakes, which they ate with gusto.

Travel was a priority for Mom. They went to Italy. Dad liked the churches, the paintings, and the food. But after three weeks, he was more than ready to be home. He was also ready to get to the cay.

Mom had decided to ration his time on the cay. That's not what she called it, but that's what it amounted to. She said one week out of four was plenty. She laid out her reasons on the phone: "He'll just rot down there. I went down and surprised him last week, and he hadn't shaved or bathed in days. He smelled like fish. The house did. Or like an old person's house."

I didn't comment that sixty-six was potentially considered old, because I knew she hadn't thought of that for a moment. She thought of herself, and Dad, as young.

"Well, he loves it down there, Mom. He can really relax."

"There's such a thing as *too* relaxed."

"Is there?" My question was not entirely rhetorical. I wanted to know her answer.

"Yes! For people like your dad, definitely! It's not his nature. He'll go crazy after a month. He needs the back and forth from here and the cay."

I did not agree but did not say it, hoping I could get off the phone and make it to a school meeting on time.

It was hard for me to imagine what he really needed in Fort Lauderdale that he couldn't find on the cay, other than Mom. Then I thought perhaps not even Mom. He had always seemed sufficient in himself, whether on the cay, at the hospital, or around the house.

We tried to meet for breakfast or lunch midway in West Palm, but my schedule remained difficult. School drop-offs, a meeting for my parish circle, the art society for Indian River County, and the day-to-day stuff meant it worked less often than not. He was careful never to push.

"You're the one running hard these days, Catherine. Whenever it works for you."

"You keep pretty busy, Dad."

"Well, this and that, you know."

"Are you writing?"

"A little. A piece on turtle grass acidity." He chuckled.

"How about poems?" I had held out hope that he would fill his time with more poetry and writing after waiting a lifetime.

"Nah. Just can't start. All the time I need, but not anything sparking."

"I know how that is. It'll come."

"Oh, yeah. Definitely. So, let's try next week. I'm on the cay this weekend. Maybe Tuesday for lunch?"

It was booked. But I been too busy the last three times. I'd move things. I told him I was free. It had been nearly a month since we had really talked, and he was not good over the phone.

We met at a place we both liked in downtown West Palm Beach near the bridge. It was light with big windows overlooking the intercoastal, and they had good oysters.

"Can mothers of three have a glass of wine before driving back to Vero?"

"Definitely."

"Good." He ordered a bottle Chardonnay and two dozen Blue Points.

He took a full report on the children and Patrick's practice, which he genuinely enjoyed hearing about. Patrick's firm was thriving. Dad wanted him to do a coffee-table book.

"It's just such beautiful work. It would be great to share it with a wider group."

"I know, it would be great. It's time. To put it together."

"Yes, the time. It's hard to find. It just goes."

Hearing that old phrase, I wanted to ask him about Sebastian and how he was holding up. But instead, I asked about Veronica.

"She's okay. Been pretty hard for her, I think. She's very private, you know, so she won't say. But there's just . . ." He stopped, put a cracker in the fish dip and held it. He looked at it for a moment in his hand. "Just a difference. Of course there is. For everyone."

He ate the cracker and had some wine. I just nodded.

"You know, they were always together. I mean, when he wasn't fishing. Around the house. Sitting on that porch. In town. Shopping, church. Really close, really good friends. The cay was something they really did together. I think she half expects him to come up that dock one late afternoon."

I had the courage to ask what I wanted to know. "What about you? How's the cay?"

"Oh, it's fine. You mean, without Sebastian?"

It was exactly what I meant, and I nodded.

"Yeah. That's hard. Pretty hard. You know. Hell, *I* half expect him to come up the dock!" He laughed a little and took a sip of wine. Then he went on, "But the flats are the hardest. I miss solving it with him. That was always so damned fun. We had a really good time."

"I know."

"Yes, you do know." He grabbed my hand and gave it a quick squeeze. He raised his eyes to the ceiling. "So the irony of my having unlimited time to fish, and missing my favorite person to fish with, is not lost on me." He laughed and shook his head.

The oysters arrived. A dozen on the half shell, and a dozen unopened. He liked to shuck some himself and slurp out the full dose of fresh, salty brine. And he was pretty proud that I could shuck them just as well after training under him.

"Ah, speaking of the sea! Here we go, Kit."

At such a moment, a thirty-five-year-old mother of three does not mind being called by her childhood nickname.

We had a couple of the shucked ones, and they were buttery and salty and lovely. He grabbed the oyster knife and the rubber grip and went to shuck one.

"Now, a really fresh one."

Mom had always fussed at him when he used knives or did yard work, saying, "A lot of money in those hands, Dr. O'Neill! Does your disability insurer know you're doing this?"

He had opened a few thousand oysters for us as children until we learned to do it for ourselves. He taught us to slip the knife in and give it a twist. He could do it without looking.

Then he struggled with that first one. He gave it a whack with the knife and tried again. His hand slipped, the oyster clattered to the table, and the knife caught the skin hard between his thumb and index finger.

He laughed out loud. "Damn!"

There was blood.

"Oh, Dad!"

"It's okay. Just slipped."

He placed the napkin around it.

"Just slipped. Good gracious! Falling apart here!"

His hands were shaking.

"I'd better stick with the half shell!"

Then he gave me the smile that he only used when a story ended badly.

CHAPTER 21

IT WAS AN EXTRAVAGANT request to make of my husband. Three days of managing the kids—the whole operation. There was a lacrosse game and a fair at the school, and he had a project meeting with an out-of-town client from Chicago.

But he knew I needed to go very much, and without the kids, or my mom.

"I've got it. You need to get down there. It's important." He smiled at me with a bit of bravery, which was much of what I loved about him.

I had not fished since Sebastian's death, and I wanted to see for myself what Dad was like on the cay now. He talked little of fishing.

I knew he often fished alone. Or with Sebastian's nephew, Joshua. I needed to see what it was like. I needed to see it for him, and for me.

So, I found myself climbing into the old Suburban at the airport on an overcast morning. He had a few days' scruff of gray beard and a good sunburn.

"North Andros Custom Car Service, ma'am." It was an old joke in our family, and I laughed and gave him a hug.

"Not shaving these days?"

"You sound like your mother. One of the luxuries of island life."

We passed the scattered houses and the little grocery. He caught me up on his projects on the cay. He had repaired the bathtub and replaced some bowed boards on the dock.

"How's Joshua?

"He's learning. He'll be very good. Already knows a lot. Really just getting to be creative with new spots, being adaptable."

He looked over at me. "You know, he knows the ones he knows. If the tide's wrong, or the moon is off, he can strike out—I don't mind—but if he's got paying customers who don't know him already, he needs to put them on fish."

I had always marveled at Sebastian's knowledge of which flat, during which tide, moon cycle, and what wind and sun would yield fish. It was like the most complex algebraic equation, with all of the solutions in the mind and eyes of an experienced bonefishing guide.

Dad added, "I strike out sometimes, too. It happens. He needed a couple more years with Sebastian. But he'll get it. It'll just take longer. Trial and error. He's a really fine young man."

I knew Joshua was older than me, but in bonefishing-guide years, he was considered young.

The wind was blowing hard from the west, and it was already midafternoon, so we would not try to fish. Dad got me settled, and we visited for a while. He wanted to hear about the children.

He went down to his shed, and I poked around the house. It

did not smell like old people the way Mom described it. But I knew Veronica had been to clean that morning, so the smell of Pine-Sol was foremost. The refrigerator also told me little, because she had put in a fresh gallon of milk, eggs, and butter, knowing that I was coming.

I found the expected stacks of books spilling around chairs and out on the veranda floor. Flies and line and a reel were on the dining room table. Though Mom had not been there for several weeks, the toile pillows were roughly in the right place. This struck me as progress in my parents' marriage.

The photos in my old room had mostly been replaced by ones of the grandchildren, and of me and my brothers grown. Kevin's wedding. Mom's sixtieth birthday dinner. One of me as a girl, with dad and my very first fish, remained. I was not sad to look at it. I was glad he was still here, puttering down in the shed, and that I was here too, with quiet and time.

When he came up from the shed, he found me sitting at the table, picking up the flies.

"You should draw some."

"Yeah. They are beautiful. But I'm not sure I need another one of bonefish flies."

"Well, it will be different this time. Right? I mean, you're different. When did you last paint one? Five, ten years ago?"

I wasn't sure, but I knew it was a long time. I'd done a number of pieces. Piles of flies on the table. Small groups of four or six. Individual ones, up close. I felt the weight of the one in my hand and thought again of the marvel of the compact body, the beauty of the feathers, and the sharp lethality of the hook hidden beneath.

He continued, "But you're different, right? You're a mom, a wife, and a fisherman. Fisherwoman." He smiled.

"But still an artist?" I smiled back.

"Yes. Always. That never leaves you."

"But more part-time now?" I was making fun of myself, but he wasn't having it.

"Part-time? No. All the time. It's always with you. I came up and found you sitting here with those flies. You don't switch on and off. Your eyes are always seeing things. Right?"

I wasn't as sure as he put it. "I suppose. But it's not conscious. I'm not thinking about painting. Or anything, really. At the moment." I laughed a little.

"Of course not. That would be overwhelming. But you see it. You admire it. You tuck it away. Or turn it over. And sometimes, it may become something. To capture, I mean."

"Is poetry that way?"

"You have to ask a poet." Now he laughed.

"But you are."

"No. It's fun. But I can't call myself that. I can't sit down and do it every day. Not like they do. I just jot."

"You call it that. But you capture things. You do. You put them down. They last."

He nodded. "Yeah, I suppose. I like to go back and read it. It reminds me of what I really thought."

"And saw," I added. "In your way."

"Yes. Very much so. My eyes. Myself, then. Imperfect. But seeking to see and render."

I decided to ask.

"Do you still see with doctor's eyes?"

He didn't mind and didn't hesitate with his word. "Yeah. Always. That's always with you."

After all these years with him and my brothers, I still wasn't sure what *that* was.

"What does that look like?"

He laughed again.

"Yeah. It's not intuitive, is it? Like your art. No, it's just a way of seeing. People. You know that they are not just the sum of the package. Not just flesh, or emotion, or actions. They're very, very complex. The whole symphony of chemistry and electrical impulse

and oxygen and light. It's either in harmony, or it's not. Bad, if it's not."
He said this last as an amused aside. "And light and wind and water,
outside. Those forces, not just chance or weather. I mean, I think
we change the way we see in school, in the early years of residency.
We see over and over and over these physical realities, causes and
effects. They can't be escaped. And they present problems to be
solved. Solving them is the thrill."

"And you miss the solving?"

"Yeah. Well, I miss a lot of it. The routines, the people, the pace.
But you can find a new construct to fill that up. But yeah, I don't have
that solving anymore. And its satisfaction and purpose."

"What fills that up?"

He clearly had not arrived at the answer yet, or he did not want
to say it. "Right now, I'm solving for dinner. We've got some grouper
I can blacken up and a big pot of peas and rice."

I agreed that sounded really good and knew we were through
talking about missing medicine.

In what was left of the afternoon, we walked in the wind the
length of the cay. He showed me where he put in some new riprap and
some plantings to slow erosion on a little jutting point. He described
the way this would thwart the steady work of the prevailing northeast
wind and current. He said he could not stop it, only slow it. Maybe
for a few years or even a decade. He looked to the northeast and
conceded that eventually the wind and water would have its way.

The next morning, Joshua was at the dock in the last of the dark.
The wind had slackened and shifted during the night as we had hoped,
though it was still blowing fifteen knots. I had a headlamp, and it shot
light around the dock and boat as we piled in our fly bags and rods.

We would take Joshua's skiff. He was very proud of it. Dad and
Sebastian had partnered with him, putting the money up for it, with
Joshua working off the amount by guiding. He owned it now after
three years. It was a beautiful Maverick 17, and even in the lamplight,
I could see that he kept it immaculately.

He said it was a falling tide, out by 9:30 AM.

"We'll run up to Mangrove Flat and see if they're in that corner?"

It was a question. Dad did not answer; he just agreed. "Yeah. Sounds like a plan."

There was a little quartering chop as we ran north, and a few splashes of spray came up on me. There was a winter chill, and I wore my fleece. The sun crept up on our right now, and the water went suddenly gold and silver. Flocks of sea ducks and gulls rose up in waves from the passing scrubby cays at our approach, arcing from the light into the remaining shadows.

I knew this flat and the way the fish stacked up in the southwest corner on occasion. But I did not know the effect of big northeast wind, or a falling tide, on this behavior. I was not sure if Joshua knew either. I was pretty certain Dad knew, but he clearly wasn't telling.

We saw no signs of fish, but the pocket was 300 yards away, and in these conditions, you could not tell. We'd have to stalk it and check for ourselves.

Joshua staked the boat, and we began our walk in. Almost immediately, we saw singles and pairs moving quickly from left to right, too fast to cast to.

Joshua pointed to them with his shark stick, and we nodded. We had seen them too. Dad paused, looked far to the right, and then continued to walk slightly behind us.

A few more pairs and singles ran around us. We got within fifty yards of the pocket and could see there was nothing. Dad was lagging far behind now, still looking to the right.

Joshua shook his head. "Nobody home." He swished the water with his stick. Dad walked up.

"Nothing?"

"No."

"Well, it's a good spot. Just not today." He looked at Joshua. "What do you think they're doing?"

"Not sure. Not here, I guess."

"Yeah. Northeast wind, tide falling out toward the wind, right?"

"Yeah." Joshua looked around the flat as if the fish might appear.

"I wonder about that edge?" Dad gestured to our right to where the flat met a broad channel. "You think they might stack up there for the bait coming out?" He posed it like a real question.

Joshua looked over at the edge and pursed his lips. "I don't know, but that might be. Let's go have a look."

It was a very long walk, and we saw singles moving through as we traveled. I had time on the walk to think about Sebastian. After a few minutes, I decided that thinking about him out here was not something I should do. Not just yet.

The edge did hold a few fish in small groups. We cast to them but had no takes. We tried changing flies, but they still weren't interested. The tide was nearly out, and the end of the flat was getting dry when we returned to the boat.

Joshua was apologetic. "I thought there'd be more here to start."

"Can't control the fish, Joshua." Dad laughed. "Next spot will be the one! "

"You're right about that, Doc!" He seemed to exhale.

The next spot was indeed good. It was a pocket that held water on the lowest tides. We had a long walk across a dry flat, but when we arrived, we saw schools of a dozen or more fish moving around in the compact area. Dad let Joshua set us up.

"We'll go from this side." He pointed to the spot. The sun and wind would be off our right shoulders, which would be okay but not ideal. Once we started in, I could see it was actually very good, because the fish began immediately moving around to our left. We wheeled slightly to work them. I caught two quickly. Joshua was very happy, and I relaxed. Dad had a refusal, then nothing.

I called to him, "Let's switch sides, Dad. They're over here."

"No, no. I'm good. Let's fish." He looked back at the fish and leaned forward, walking slowly closer to them.

He had a long cast to reach them, and they were a little spooked.

He took a few strokes, then let go. It was too long, and the line slapped hard on the school. There was an explosion of water, and they fled, rocketing off in a dozen directions.

"Agh! Sorry, guys."

The remaining fish moved left very quickly, then away. He slapped his rod tip on the water, then turned back toward the boat. I caught up with him.

"Tough break."

"Yeah. Not a break. Bad cast. Just a little too much."

"It happens."

"Yeah." He shook his head. He turned to me and brightened, adding, "But two nice fish for you!"

"Yeah, well, not bad for a full-time mom!"

He laughed, and we walked on to the boat.

Through the course of the day, I watched him miss more than I had seen him miss in all the years we had fished together. It didn't help that we saw only a few good groups, and those we did see were not feeding aggressively.

The wind picked up to twenty-five knots by midafternoon, and a line of thunderstorms stacked up to the northeast. Joshua wanted to fish on.

"Let's just try this next one at Crab Cay."

Dad looked up at the approaching storm clouds, then back at Joshua. "I think we've had about enough. Weather looks like it's turning."

"It's not far. Let's just check it."

Dad turned back to the boat. "Okay."

When we got to the south flat at Crab, the wind was howling, and the dark clouds had obscured the sun. The flat was dancing with waves and wind. I looked at Dad and smiled, but he did not smile back. He was scanning the water. I wasn't sure if he was gauging the weather or looking for fish.

Joshua began to stake the boat. I thought all of this was unnecessary.

"So, we're doing this?"

Joshua looked up. "Just give it a few minutes?"

Dad said nothing. He just grabbed his rod and hopped out into the knee-deep water.

We followed Joshua up onto the flat, and then turned to put the wind to our backs. We could see nothing in the water but wind swirls and white caps. I was walking close enough to Dad to quietly say, "This is stupid, Dad. We aren't going to see any fish."

He kept looking straight ahead.

"Come on, Catherine. Let's fish."

We kept walking. But it was not fishing. We finished stalking the flat, having seen nothing. We turned back to the boat. The first wave of thunderstorms was nearly upon us, the sky black and the wind blowing hard in our faces. Dad turned to Joshua to say, "I think we better get back, Joshua."

"Yeah. Looks bad."

I wanted to add that yes, it had looked bad for well over an hour, but I did not. We walked quickly to the boat, and Dad unstaked it while Joshua turned the boat away from the flat. The wind pushed back, and he struggled.

He ran us quickly south, at full throttle through dark channels in the failing light. The water was kicked up and whitecapping. The storm was on top of us, and rain pelted hard and the wind stung our faces and hands. I was cold and very wet.

I heard Dad next to me say, "Lovely day for a boat ride, ma'am." It was another of our old jokes from my childhood, and I laughed and stuck my elbow into his ribs. He tilted his head back and smiled up at dark clouds above. I was glad to see his real smile, thinking he was okay despite the way the day had gone.

He had not caught a single fish. I caught five. Joshua was worried it was a bad day. At the dock, we assured him it was not, and certainly not his fault. Difficult conditions. The fish were not feeding. He seemed to feel better by the time he pulled away from the cay.

That night, Dad grilled the steaks I'd brought from home in the cooler, and we had a bottle of very good red wine Patrick sent along for dad. I told him to save it, but he wasn't having it. "How many special occasions do you think I have out here?"

We talked about how Joshua had done that day. Dad was not critical. "Oh, he's fine. He still learning. He'll be very good."

"Did you know that first pocket at Mangrove would be empty? And that the fish would be on that other edge?"

He nodded. "Yeah. I thought so."

"Why didn't you tell him?"

"Well, it's not . . . It's not my place. I mean, he might have been right. And he's got to learn it. I can't just tell him. He's the guide. I need to let him be the guide."

"Would you have told Sebastian?"

"I wouldn't have had to tell Sebastian."

"But you'd suggest things."

"Well, yeah. And he was polite enough to consider them. But he was so far ahead of me. I was always still learning."

"I thought of you as peers."

He shook his head and smiled a little. "No. More like master and pupil. Maybe professor and grad student." He laughed again.

"I know you miss him."

"Oh, yeah." He looked around the big room. "You know, it's almost worse here. He's not around to fish. He's not on the flats." He paused and looked at the candles. "I liked being here alone all these years. I mean, I liked it when you all and Mom would come. But I also enjoyed the quiet and solitude. But now, I realized it's because it was always broken up. Sebastian and Veronica were always around, popping in. You guys would be over. I had a lot less *alone* than I thought."

"Mom likes coming over."

"Yeah, I think she does. It's been nice."

"Would you rather be here or at home?"

I really wanted to know. He raised his eyebrows and smiled. "Tough one." He considered for another moment, continuing, "Oh, I don't know. I go a little crazy at home. But I'm just a little sad here right now. You know, just a little something missing. Not the same. Not sure if it's you kids all grown up or what. Something. I don't know. This place is the people too. And they're not here."

He shook his head. He looked directly at me. "I missed a lot today."

It was true. But I said, "No. Tough conditions. Hard to see. Hard to cast."

"No. I just missed. I've been missing. A lot."

"Everybody has bad days."

"Yeah. But not all of them."

I was flat-footed by this and didn't know what to say. I waited several beats too long. Then he was up and clearing his place.

"Veronica brought some guava duff. How about coffee?"

I told him that those both sounded good. We did the dishes together, listening to The Royals, talking about subjects he enjoyed, my children and my husband's architectural practice.

We had agreed with Joshua that if the weather allowed, we would fish again the next day. But the weather did not relent. It blew up during the night, and thunderstorms stacked up the whole next day. I left the cay on Sunday in a heavy chop, with hard rain and wind howling from the northeast.

I looked back to see Dad on the dock in his yellow raincoat and ball cap. He gave a big wave and turned back to walk up to the house.

CHAPTER 22

BECAUSE I HAD SAID I wanted to see for myself, Mom insisted on a full report. She caught me the next Tuesday after I returned. I'd just done the school drop-off and was cleaning up the mess from breakfast. She rang the house phone, then my cell. Twice. I picked up the second time and sat down at the kitchen table.

"Well, what did you think? Did it smell like old people?"

I had to smile and laugh at this. She went on, "Admit it. He needs to know."

"No, Mom. Smelled great, like Pine-Sol."

"The house or your dad?"

I laughed. "Both. It was really nice. We had a chance to catch up."

She would never stop at something that simple. "Well, how was he? How did he look? Grizzled?"

"He looked fine, Mom. You should go see."

"Oh, he cleans up for me. Totally different if I'm there. I wanted to see what he's like in his native state."

"Not very native. He seemed fine. I mean, he could use a little company."

"Your father? We're talking about Jack O'Niell? The great lone bonefish hunter, poet, and . . ." She stopped herself and finished with uncomfortable laugh.

"Yeah, exactly. *Not* surgeon. He could use a little company, Mom."

"He hasn't said that. He likes it there alone. I always feel like he's waiting for me to go home."

"Well, things change. I mean, there's a lot of change right now for him."

"Oh, goodness, Catherine. He is absolutely fine. Your father does not *need* someone to fix him. Or to be there with him. He's not built like that."

When I was in school, I was surprised to find out that no one else's father spent time away like my dad. They might play golf and go on golf weekends. Or hunt and go on hunting trips. Or even fish a lot and go away to fish. But no one had a dad that took regular long weekends alone. Or weeks fishing with just visits from his wife and family. At least, no one whose parents were in love. But I was always sure they were in love.

As I got older and found out what love is, I found out this was rare. But whatever they did seemed to work for them. So, I had stopped spending much time wondering how it worked.

Now I was thirty-five years old, and I had been married for nine years to someone I loved. I couldn't imagine being away for a week, or many weekends. She seemed to be in a good mood, and I wanted to know, so I asked, "How has it worked? I mean, him being at the cay so much? Didn't you miss him? Miss each other?"

"Yeah, we did. I did. Of course. But it was important for him. He needed it. We worked it out."

"How? I mean, were you upset? Or frustrated?"

"It was hard. We fought over it. But we worked it out."

I recalled the No Money Cay conversations. But they seemed lighthearted. And I was little. I also recalled her tone about the cay. When he returned, she didn't listen long to any stories of how his time had been there. She changed the subject immediately to what we had been doing. The boys' sports. My ballet and art. Or her projects around the house. They must have kept the arguing behind closed doors.

"What did he need? I mean, that you couldn't give. Or we couldn't?"

"Oh, I don't know. Not that. What is it? Peace. Solitude. I don't know. He gave so much every day, all week. All hours, always. To his patients. It was all-consuming. Whatever he had left, we soaked up. He would get so . . ." She paused. "It was almost like . . . hollowed out. There just wasn't anything left of him. When he started going over to fish, I really resented it. Taking the little time he had on that. But he was changed when he got back. He was much more like himself. Then, pretty soon, the boys went with him. Then you. It was special. Really good times. He just glowed when he came back. He was whole again. I don't know, it's hard to explain."

She stopped then, and it was very quiet on the phone. And she finished what she had to say. "He's complicated, Catherine. More complicated than you think."

I did not think of him that way. But she sounded right. I just said, "Uh-huh."

And she went on, "So, he's had his time. He needed it. And he had it. We're in a different place now. There are things I need to do. And want to do. And he's doing those things. It all works out."

I knew he was traveling with her. They had to been to Spain, Portugal, New York, and San Francisco in the last three months.

There were lots of plans for more. But he never talked about the trips, before or after. It felt to me a little like a penance.

"Is he paying you back? I thought good marriages didn't count or keep track?"

This had been her advice many times. She laughed at hearing it back.

"It's not counting. We've both given. Freely. He is giving. That's what you do, Catherine."

"I'm worried about him, Mom."

"I know you are, honey. But I know him. He's okay. He is making a big adjustment. That doesn't just happen. He's going to be fine. Give him some time."

I did give it time. I immersed myself in my own family and painted when I could, and months tracked by. I saw photos of a trip to New Zealand. Mom loved it. He spoke about it with some enthusiasm. But this was probably not a fair test since Mom had booked three days of trout fishing at a lodge on the South Island. He thought the fishing was easy, but the fish were beautiful, and the setting was spectacular. And he said he liked the wine.

He seemed downright cheerful when he came up for one of John's lacrosse games. He had a big hat and some zinc smeared on his face. I could picture him on the flats. He was headed over the next day for a week. Mom would join him the following week. He seemed excited.

"I've got a new 9 weight that throws much truer. Excited to try it. The weather looks spectacular."

I told him I wished I could join him.

"You should! Bring the kids."

I shook my head. School would not allow it.

"Forget about school. Gets in the way of all the fun."

In that moment, he almost seemed like an ordinary grandfather, watching his grandson, talking about his travels, and excited to go fishing.

CHAPTER 23

MY BROTHERS WERE BOTH consumed with their practices and with their wives and children. Kevin and I had lunch once in a while. Or talked on the phone. Charlie did not return calls or texts. He'd apologize when we finally caught up.

So when I saw Charlie's phone come up on my cell twice in quick succession, I took a pan off the stove and picked up. He sounded out of breath, and he cut out. Something about Dad. He was laughing a little but did not sound amused.

"Where are you?"

"Oh, sorry. At the hospital, walking up the stairs in the parking garage." He dropped again.

He called back a moment later.

"Sorry, can you hear me?"

"Yeah. What's up?" I looked at the boats passing by in the intercoastal channel out of the kitchen window.

"It's about Dad. Mom wants me to go over there."

I wasn't understanding, and he kept blanking out.

"Charlie, this is a bad connection. What about Dad?"

He blanked out again and then ". . . lost on the flats."

"I didn't hear you. What?"

"Dad, he got lost on the flats." He gave another chuckle that did not sound funny.

"Lost? I don't—"

"No, it's okay. He's fine. But Mom wants me to go over. You know, to talk to him."

"Dad can't get lost. I'm not—"

"No, no. Well, I don't know. He says he got stuck on a sandbar, but he was gone all night. Joshua found him out there the next day. Way up in the northern Joulters."

I felt dizzy thinking of my dad lost in the Joulters. Or stuck. It wasn't possible. There was a mistake.

"I don't . . . I mean . . . I don't see how that could happen, Charlie."

"Yeah, well, it did. So, I'm heading over this afternoon. Mom asked me to let you know."

"I'm going too."

"No, it's okay. You've got too much going on, Catherine."

"No, I can do it."

"I don't think there's a seat. I took the last one. Well, actually, they did me a favor and bumped someone for Staniel."

"So, what are you going to do? He's fine, right?"

"Yeah, well, he's at the cay. He's okay. Mom just wants me to go check on him. Talk to him." He paused. "I think he's pretty upset."

I hung up and checked with Makers Air. I knew the girl at the desk. They had four on the waiting list. They'd cleared the seat for Charlie as a favor. The girl said, "Medical emergency."

I called Charlie back.

"I talked to Makers. Medical emergency?"

"I just told them that. It's not. Just needed to get over and see him. You know Mom's all in a tizzy."

"Why isn't she going?"

"He didn't want Mom. Said she shouldn't come. Not a big deal, you know? She's respecting that. She's going down in three days, anyway. Don't worry. This is no big deal. I'll give you a full report."

Charlie did not give me a full report. He and Dad flew home together the next day. When I arrived at Mom and Dad's house, Charlie was still there. I found him with Dad in his study. Charlie's face was red. Dad was sitting in the corner in his big reading chair. He looked tired. I went to hug him.

"Oh my goodness. You came down for this?"

"I'm glad you're okay."

"Okay?" He looked at Charlie with irritation. "For Pete's sake, I got stuck on a sandbar." He looked to Charlie again. "What have you and your mother been telling everyone? Good gracious! I'm fine. Call out the Coast Guard, for Pete's sake!"

He shook his head. Charlie wasn't smiling. He stood up.

"Just worried about you, Dad."

"Well, don't. I'm fine."

Charlie raised his eyebrows at me and walked out of the room. I heard him talk to Mom, and then heard the front door. I looked at Dad and smiled our old co-conspirators' smile. "So, what's going on?"

He shook his head again. "Stuck on a bar. Could happen to anyone, as you know." I did not agree because he had never been stuck on a bar.

"Where?"

"Oh, up north." He did not name the flat, and I did not ask. "Anyway, they think I got lost. I was certainly not lost."

He stopped and looked out into the room. He turned back to me.

"Your mother's totally overreacting. And Charlie too."

I left him there and found Mom on the back terrace. She was just sitting. I sat down next to her.

"So, what's going on?"

"Well, you know as much as I do. He got lost. He was gone all night. I was worried sick. Veronica was worried. Had half of North Andros looking for him."

"He said he got stuck."

"You believe that? Has he ever been stuck?"

I shook my head. "But he's also never been lost. I mean, in the Joulters. He knows them like the back of his hand."

She turned and looked directly at me. "And that's why I'm worried."

I called Charlie on my way home. It went to voicemail, but he called me back a minute later.

"Sorry, I was talking to Kevin."

"What does he think?"

"About what?"

"About Dad?"

"I was just filling him in."

"So, what do you think, Charlie?"

"About what happened?"

"Yeah. And Dad. I mean, is he okay?"

"He was very dehydrated. A little disoriented. He was in pretty bad shape when I got there."

"Do you think he got lost?"

"I don't know. I don't. Hard to tell. I just know he spent a day and night out on the Joulters, and it was probably pretty unpleasant."

"What did Joshua say?"

"Not much. He just said he's glad Dad's okay. Couldn't tell me much. Or wouldn't."

"Wouldn't?"

"Well, yeah. I mean, he's Dad's guy. Who knows what Dad told him? He's not going to rat Dad out with his kids."

"What did Dad tell you?"

"That he got stuck."

"Where?"

"Up north."

"Nothing more specific?"

"Nope. And I didn't ask."

"Me either." We were quiet.

Then I said what we both thought, "Maybe because we're afraid he wouldn't know."

It was quiet again. Then I heard Charlie's voice over the phone and couldn't tell what his expression was. "Yeah. Well, this is hard." He paused. "Mom doesn't want him to fish alone anymore."

I snorted. "What? That's ridiculous. He's been fishing alone for thirty years."

"Yeah, but he had Sebastian. Or us."

"He fished alone a lot, Charlie."

"I know. But things change."

"You're not actually considering this? Telling Dad he can't fish alone?"

"I already did."

It was the conversation I had interrupted. And it was why Charlie's face was red when I walked in. Dad was furious. He refused to even consider it. It was a question for him alone. Not even Mom had a say in it.

"And I've asked him to get some tests."

"What tests?"

"Neurological. I'm a little concerned. I want to at least get a baseline."

"For what?"

"He's off. I'm not sure. But he's off. And he's . . . I don't know, he's a little . . . it's not tracking, Catherine. For sixty-six, it's not making sense. All of it just has my antenna up. You know?"

"Your son antenna, or your doctor antenna?"

"There is no difference. Not on this, Catherine." It was what Dad would have said.

"So, is he going to do it?"

"Nope. Not if we let him decide. Flat refuses. Said it's ridiculous. Said he knows himself."

"Physician, heal thyself."

He didn't laugh, just grunted. "Yeah. It's funny how true that is." He paused again. "So, Mom was going to get him to calm down and talk to him."

All I could manage before we hung up was "Well, good luck with that."

Luck would not be enough. He would not get any tests done. Or even discuss any of it with Charlie or Kevin. If he would not talk to my medical brothers, I thought he might talk to me. But he would not. I brought it up three times in the months that followed, and he briskly changed the subject in a way I knew meant the subject was closed.

He would not be tested. And he would not fish alone. At least, if he wanted to stay married. Mom put her foot down and forbade him from fishing without Joshua or her or someone.

I'd never seen her give him an ultimatum. Perhaps she never had. But she gave this one, and he obeyed. In his own way, of course.

He fished less. He only went once in the months that followed, one day with her and Joshua. When he came back and I asked him about it, he said the fishing had been poor. Mom said they'd had a great time.

When Mom came up the following week to see the kids, she seemed rattled and unsteady in a way I had never seen before. When I asked her what was wrong, she brightly replied, "Nothing, just a little tired," and moved on.

But I would not let her go. Just as she was getting ready to leave, I asked her to sit with me. I looked directly at her. "Mom, I'm a little worried. You seem out of sorts. Dad seems out of sorts. What's going on?"

She pursed her lips. She started to speak, but then stopped, and put her hand to her lips. "Your father . . ." Her voice caught. She started again, "Your father is . . ."

"What, Mom?"

"He's having a *hard* time, Kit." Tears welled up in her eyes. I put my hand on her hands.

"What is it, Mom?"

"I don't know. He won't talk about it."

"Well, I mean, is he sick?"

"I don't know. I don't. It's just . . . he's . . ."

She looked up at the ceiling and blinked out tears. She couldn't find the words and just shook her head. "He's mad at me. For not letting him fish. Alone. He's blaming that on me. He's not himself. Forgetting, arguing. It's not just aging . . . if he'd just get some tests . . . but he says he doesn't need any tests. He won't listen to Charlie or Kevin."

"Or me."

"Or you. Or me." She laughed a little now.

"I'm sure it's nothing. Just getting used to this new life." She gave a quick nod. It seemed like a nod to confirm it to herself.

CHAPTER 24

I TRIED ONE MORE TIME. I asked him over for coffee, just the two of us. I told him it would make me feel better. This time, he did not brush me off. Instead, he explained to me carefully and precisely that he knew himself better than anyone. As a physician, and as someone who was very aware of his own body, he did not need any tests to tell him whether he was well—or ill.

He was right about this last thing. He did not need any tests to know what was wrong. He had diagnosed himself within three months of the full onset of symptoms—sudden and acute episodic memory loss, a weakness in his hands and extremities, a loss of motor coordination, an episodic loss of vision, disorientation, and fatigue. He kept his diagnosis to himself until he was quite certain.

It was a rare neurological disorder that attacked the central nervous system suddenly and aggressively. It had a peculiar hyphenated Swiss name, named after the two researchers who identified it in the 1950s. I never bothered to learn the name. I didn't need to. It was just the disease that was killing my father.

Swiftly. There was no treatment. He faded before our eyes. His weight loss made him seem smaller each time I saw him. His memory loss pulled him away from us day by day.

But in those last few weeks, we all had a chance to see him as he really was. On certain days, he was very lucid, very sharp. He spent time with each of us on those good days.

He sat in a big chair in a patch of morning sunshine in the family room. He said he had nothing left to teach me, that I learned all the lessons he had for me. I was the best at really listening, really seeing—the way he always pictured his children would. Then he smiled at me, the same smile he always gave me as a child when a lesson was complete. "So, now you have everything you need, Kit."

It was a very warm smile. I could not say anything. My tongue was thick. I did not trust my eyes. Mom told us that he did not want a lot crying. So I just nodded.

"It's okay. This is part of it. Right? Now you and I have had a lifetime of looking for the true thing, haven't we? We've been pursuing that. This . . . this is my next step. I'm going to maybe see it now. Right? It's what's next."

Then he hugged me and held me out, looking at me and smiling again. He was tearing up a little. "So, that's where I'll be." Then he was not teary anymore. "Now, you remember what I told you."

I nodded and managed to say it: "Clear eyes, steady hand."

He laughed and hugged me again—this time, very tightly.

"That's right. You have everything you need."

He kept a notebook to record his symptoms, to document what he sensed caused them. When he got weaker, he spoke into a small tape recorder. He was adamant that this last work might be a helpful case study to those seeking a cure.

When he felt strong enough, he went to early-morning Mass at St. Anthony's with Mom. He spent time putting his books in order. And sorting through fishing gear and the things he wanted us to have.

He refused hospice and a ventilator or any pain medication. He said he did not want to dull this last part or miss any of the passage ahead.

When the final days came, he wanted to go to the cay. But we had waited a day too long. He declined rapidly and could not travel.

That afternoon, he drifted into sleep. We sat around the bed, taking turns wiping his brow and holding his hand. We prayed the Rosary. In the end, Mom opened the big windows, and we felt the warm, salty air fill the room, and he was gone.

My mom had often said that funerals are for the living, and I saw how true that was the next week. The pace of finalizing obituaries, the funeral home, receiving friends and family, and planning for the funeral Mass was constant and busy. Out-of-town family arrived, we took sympathy calls from friends, and we had very little time to grieve.

Veronica came with Malcolm and Freddy. They stayed at my aunt Angie's house a few blocks away. They came to the house before the wake. Veronica hugged us all and shook her head. "It's been a very hard year," she said, a thought we all agreed with. She gave Mom the biggest and longest hug, and told her it would be all right, and that "those two men" were together again. Joshua and six other Andros men came to the funeral. I thought one might be the man I saw Dad save.

Mom brought her formidable determination to doing everything the right way, in the way Dad would have wanted. This constant work meant that the four of us did not have a chance to really sit together until after the graveside service in the old yard beside St. Anthony's, after the last of the visiting family had left for the airport.

It was only 3 PM, but Charlie and Kevin and I poured a rum,

and Mom had a glass of wine. A lot of very kind things had been said about our father that week, so we did not say those things again.

Instead, we talked a little about the friends and relatives we caught up with. Our spouses were in and out of the room, chasing children, offering a thought. We decided that Dad would've liked the Mass and services.

We raised our glasses to him one time together, and it was my brother Kevin who was strong enough to say, "Clear eyes and a steady hand," so we could all smile just a little.

CHAPTER 26

I FOUND MOM clearing out his closet, piling up old clothes and hangers. I started to help, but she told me she had a system, and I was messing up her piles. I sat down on the dressing chair in the corner as she worked.

"Can you believe all of this? I mean, how many shirts does a man need? He wore a white shirt and lab coat every day for forty years, and an old fishing shirt the rest the time. What are all these?" She threw a stack of multicolor pastels and prints on top of a pile on the floor.

"What are you going to do with all this, Mom?"

"See if the boys or Patrick want any of it. Everything else goes to the St. Vincent de Paul."

She did not look at me when she said any of this. She just kept grabbing hangers and adding to the piles of clothes.

"I'm sure there are some nice things."

"Well, go through it and see what you want."

"Mom?" She kept working and did not look at me.

"Mom?" She stopped and looked over.

"Are you going to keep anything? Any of this?"

"Well, not the clothes. It doesn't do any good here. I mean, the books and things and fishing gear. You know what he wanted."

I did know. He told us with precision about who would get which of the reels and rods, and which books were special.

I looked at the empty racks in the closet they'd shared for thirty years. I did not ask her what she was going to put in that empty space.

When she finished, we carried the piles downstairs, and she washed the dust from her hands and face in the kitchen sink. I made a pot of coffee. We sat at the kitchen table where the midday light from the big windows to the backyard fell on us.

She asked about the children and told me about her garden club project at a local park. Then we were both quiet. She played with her ring, turning it on her finger.

When she looked up, I asked her, "So, how are you doing, Mom?"

"Fine. How are you? I'm worried about you and your brothers."

"We're fine. We're dealing with it. We miss him. It's hard. You know."

"Yeah. Well, that's good. We just have to deal with it. That's what he'd want."

She took a sip of coffee and held the mug to her lips.

"I'm just . . . oh . . ."

I saw tears welling in her eyes.

"It's okay, Mom. This is so hard."

She gave me her brave smile. "No, it's not. It's not. It's part of things. Didn't he tell you that?" She put the coffee down and crossed her arms. She looked down and shook her head.

"He had all the answers. Your father."

I did not know what to say.

"I was so sure we would have more time." She gave a humorless chuckle. "But everyone says that, right? There was so much I waited to do. So much we had *planned* to do. I had given and waited, and this was just not fair. Who doesn't get tested? Who doesn't go to the doctor?"

"Mom, there was nothing that could have been done. You know that."

"Yes. The Kriegstadten, Kreegstoudt, whatever it is. I've heard all about it. Untreatable, right? But what if he finds out a year earlier? What else could have been done? What else could we have done as a family? And the time? That time belonged to me, too, to all of us. You know, this is just so typical of him. That certainty, that stubborn, single-minded . . . so *sure* all the time. Never asking anyone else."

She gave a snort and shook her head.

"You can't blame this on him, Mom. It just happened."

"I'm not blaming him. It's just . . . I just thought . . . there are things *I* wanted. Now it's just . . ."

She wiped the tears away and shook her head again, getting up for more coffee. I went up and gave her a hug, but she felt stiff, hardly hugging me back.

A month later, I felt it was time and called to offer to go to the cay the next weekend and clear out Dad's things for her. I thought it would save her the emotion I had seen at the house. But she was ready for me. "Yes, it would be good to get things cleaned up. We need to get it in shape to sell."

All I could manage was "Sell? Sell what?" I actually thought she meant the clothes.

"The cay. I spoke to a broker in Nassau. Thinks it will sell very quickly. These private islands are apparently very sought after."

"We can't sell the cay. Come on, Mom." I sat down with the phone.

"No. I've decided, Catherine. It's the right thing to do. You have to trust me on these things. It's just going to sit there. We have to be practical."

"Practical? It's our home. I mean, how can we sell it?"

"It's not our home. I'm sitting in our home. Our family home. I don't need an island in The Bahamas. You don't have time to use it. Your brothers certainly don't have time to use it. Come on, Catherine, let's be smart now."

"What about the boys? What do they say about all this?"

"They agree." She was quiet for a moment. "I know you love it, we all love it, but it's just not practical to keep it. You know it's expensive, Catherine. It doesn't just run on fishing."

"Is this about money? I mean, Mom, I thought—"

"No, no. I'm fine. Dad left me very well taken care of. I just don't need two houses. No one does."

It took me three unreturned calls, but that evening, I got ahold of Charlie. He was helping Mom settle Dad's affairs. He was also ready. "Yeah. I know. But it's Mom's choice. It's her call, Catherine."

"What about Dad's choice? He would never want it sold."

"I don't know. I didn't talk to him about it. Did you?"

I had never even thought to ask.

"No. I wouldn't ask him that. It's really not my business."

"Exactly. It's between Dad and Mom. I'm sure they talked about it."

"I doubt it."

"Really?"

"I think Mom's mad at Dad."

"Mad? What are you talking about?"

"Doesn't she seem angry?"

"She just lost her husband, Catherine. Give her a break."

I closed the conversation with an irritable remark about not lecturing me about Elisabeth Kübler-Ross and hung up.

When I called Kevin, I caught him in the middle of rounds. He quickly cut me off and said that it was Mom's call, and then got off the phone in response to voices in the background at the hospital.

When Patrick came home from work, he found me pacing in his study. The kids were watching TV. There was no sign of dinner.

"Hey, you okay?"

"No." I looked down and shook my head with my arms crossed.

"I'm sorry. What is it?"

"Mom's selling the cay."

"Oh my." He shook his head. He put his case down, walked away to order pizzas, then fixed us both a large rum drink. I told him the whole story.

"So, everybody agrees."

"Except you?"

"Except me."

"And me. Well, actually, I'm okay with your Mom selling it."

"What? How can you say that?"

"Well, it's okay for her to sell it. If we can buy it."

I looked at him like he was crazy. "What are you talking about?"

"We buy it. Makes perfect sense."

"Did you have drinks before you left the office? We don't have the money for that."

"Well, I'm sure your Mom will give us a discount."

"Yeah right."

"A little one." He held his thumb and forefinger up close together and smiled.

"Come on, Patrick. We've got kids to take care of."

"I think we can do it. Firm's going good. And I want to do it. It's a very special place. I met a really amazing girl there once." He laughed and smiled broadly.

"This is not your dream, Patrick. What about the house down in the keys? The lots you've been looking at? The drawings. What about all of that?"

"Ah, this is my dream. All that is not important. This is important.

I love that house. *We* love that house." I looked at him and knew he wasn't just being kind—he was telling the truth.

We ate some pizza and put the kids to bed. We spent the evening drinking some very good red wine and doing the kind of math you do with someone you love when you very much want to make a thing come true.

Just before bed, he told me that college for the kids was just optional anyway. I punched him in the ribs and told him I still thought he was crazy, but I was glad he was insane enough to do this with me.

I called Mom the next day to tell her.

"You're what?"

"We want to buy the cay."

"Oh, come on, Kit. That makes no sense. You don't even have time to go there."

"We will. We'll make time. It's a great place for the kids." Then, to hurt her, I added, "Just like us."

Characteristically, she ignored this.

"Do you know how much it's going to sell for?"

"Yeah. I have a pretty good idea. I would hope for a little discount." I laughed a little, but she did not laugh.

"No. It's got to be a fair price. Whatever the broker says. This is for your brothers too. Market price."

"Okay. We're ready."

She did not agree, and we hung up.

Two days later, she called and asked me to come down and see her, told me not to bring Patrick. She said we needed to talk about the cay.

She was sitting in the living room when I came in, in a blouse and pearls. She was looking through an old scrapbook. I could see that it was photos of our childhood, and she quickly closed it.

"I want to talk to you about the cay. About your father. I want to have a real talk about this."

I sat down across from her on the couch and said, "Okay."

"You know I didn't want it. To buy it. To go there. It was not my thing. It was your father's."

I nodded.

"Okay." She looked down at her lap and smoothed her skirt, and then looked directly at me. "So, the cay is not a thing I want. I love that you love it. I loved that he loved it. But it does not make me happy to be there. It does not bring me good to be there."

"What about us? I mean, we all went there as kids. With you and Dad."

"Yes, I know. But I can't imagine going there. I can't imagine being there and it being a good thing. He's not there. You won't be there. It's empty. It's not a happy thing for me."

"But he loved it."

"He did. He loved it very much."

It was quiet for a moment. Then I said, looking her in the eyes, "And so do I."

She shook her head. "Oh, Kit. He's not there. You think you'll like being there?"

"Yes. It makes me happy to be there. To me, he is there. He'll always be there for me."

She looked at me for a long moment. Then she nodded once. "Okay. I see. It's okay." She said it almost to herself. Then she looked up at me and said, "Well, let's see. It's an awful lot of money. I don't want to see you and Patrick strapped."

"Well, how about a family discount?" I smiled.

She laughed a little for the first time in a long while.

"I'll have to convince your brothers. Or *you* will."

We got a discount, but it wasn't much. So we scraped and borrowed and somehow made it work. Mom said the best part was not having to go move everything out, and I think she meant that.

The week after we closed, Patrick and I went down with the kids. I boxed up Dad's clothes and left the fishing gear and books for another time. The children played on the beach as we put fresh paint on the family room walls, and Patrick mended some broken boards on the veranda.

Joshua brought Veronica out. She brought a hamper of food and a housewarming gift. It was an architect's drawing table. Freddy had found it in an old house in Nicholls Town and restored it. The cherrywood and Andros pine were rich and bright. Patrick put it in the main room, looking out the big windows to the reef.

Veronica looked around at the big room and the fresh paint and let out a big, contented sigh. We could hear the children laughing out on the beach. She smiled and shook her head a little, laughing gently. "This reminds me so much of another time, moving in. Sebastian and I here to help. Your mom and dad were so young! You and your brothers. A very happy time."

I got a little teary, but for the first time in a long time, it was the happy kind. I nodded and gave her a very big hug.

We had casting practice with the kids in the late afternoon, and I made sure it was fun. We quit early, and there were no tears. Then Patrick grilled the crawfish Veronica had brought. The children devoured the crawfish and her baked mac and cheese. We put the children to bed.

Then we sat together in the rope hammock we'd strung on the veranda and looked up at the very big stars. I thanked him for buying the house. He laughed and told me I was very expensive—but also very worth it.

I came back to the cay the next month. Patrick wanted to come too, but the children were busy with school, and we could not find a sitter for three days. Mom was on what she called a "widow invite"— staying with some good friends at their house in the mountains. I invited her to come to the cay, but we agreed that she needed Colorado and the cool air more.

My chest still ached when I woke each day, and for the first time, I was a little afraid of the house alone. Joshua took me out, and Veronica got me settled. After they left, the weather turned dark and the wind howled, with dark-gray clouds building in the east. A storm came through and was gone in a half hour, leaving the reef and cay in a brief patch of golden light. There was another band of dark clouds approaching with the shadow of heavy rain beneath it, and I watched it roll toward me.

I knew it was time. I had painted all over North Andros and on the cay, but I had never painted the flats to the north that I loved so much. I had never had the courage to try and capture the high, bright sky, the vast white flats stretching to the sea, and the sheer immensity and color of it all.

That day, I knew that I was enough of a fisherman to see it, and enough of a painter to capture it. I had everything I needed.

The weather would not allow me to go out into it, but when I thought of the flats, I knew I did not need to go. I could clearly see the vast white flat and the edges of many blues, greens, and grays. I mixed the paints and chose my biggest canvas.

I worked very hard and well and completed it that last afternoon—two distant figures crossing the flat slowly and carefully, leaning slightly forward, searching and seeing. When it was finished, I knew that—with paint and light and brush and line—I had found what I was looking for. My chest ached a little less when I woke in the morning. I took the painting home with me. I would not sell this one. It was just for me.

So, I am comforted now to know that while my father's body may rest in the old cemetery beside St. Anthony's, I can still find him there, on the other side of the Gulf Stream, in the late-afternoon sun, far across an endless flat, walking slowly, line singing, eyes clear, hands steady, pursuing one true moment in paradise.

CPSIA information can be obtained
at www.ICGtesting.com
Printed in the USA
JSHW012302281122
34004JS00002B/176